NIGHT OFFICE

ASSET RESOURCE MANAGEMENT

FOR INTERNAL USE ONLY

NIGHT OFFICE

IN THE MANSION OF MADNESS

COMPILED BY MARK TEPPO

ASSET RESOURCE MANAGEMENT

PAE–138/b   FOR INTERNAL USE ONLY

51325 Books

Produced in association with **51325 Books** and Firebird Creative, LLC (Clackamas, OR).

But what if I chose the wrong path?

A Night Office publication
ARM – PAE – 138/b
rev. 43 / ed. 01.2020

ASSET RESOURCE MANAGEMENT

IN THE MANSION
OF MADNESS

PAE-138/b　　　　　　FOR INTERNAL USE ONLY

SCOPE: This psychological assessment exercise is a training manual used by Night Office Asset Resource Management. The exercise creates a psychological matrix that encapsulates the mental acuity, psychological stability, and intellectual resourcefulness of a potential Night Office field operative candidate.

Given the complex nth-dimensional sub-structures of the psychological matrices developed by the Night Office, assessment scores given by these exercises are merely a cursory summation of a potential candidate's qualifications. Further assessment may be required before a candidate can be considered for a Night Office field operative position.

Night Office Asset Resource Management makes every effort to keep these training manuals in accordance with the most current policies, procedures, and practical applications of relevant esoteric knowledge, but Night Office Asset Resource Management offers no assurances that materials are truly up-to-date.

AUDIENCE: The intended audience for this psychological assessment exercise are candidates who have passed preliminary screening for Night Office field operative positions. All candidates must have the Standard Non-Disclosure Agreement on record (Form PALM—DLT—23/d).

Prior to completing the psychological assessment exercise, candidates must read & initial a Psychological Evaluation Awareness Form (PALM—ISA—84/b) and a Living Will Agreement Form (PALM—WRL—54/q).

NOTE: Night Office Asset Resource Managment will factor in the number of times a candidate has attempted to complete this psychological assessment exercise as part of their summary judgement. The candidate should not trouble themselves with how Night Office Asset Resourec Management knows this data. All summary judgements by Night Office Asset Resource Management are final.

A judgement of DNH by Night Office Asset Resource Management is valid for one (1) year. Candidates may be reevaluated when the DNH notation expires.

DISCLAIMER: This psychological assessment exercise is intended to familiarize potential field operative candidates with workplace hazards, mental health stressors, and other psychological complexities that may present themselves during the course of performing designated Night Office tasks. While Night Office Asset Resource Management has attempted to thoroughly address all possible scenarios and outcomes of these psychological assessment exercises, it is entirely likely that new stressors, hazards, and other causes for psychotic breaks may present themselves as a result of, or during the process of, or in the aftermath of completing this exercise. To the extend that local, state, and federal guidelines, mandates, and statutes regarding extra-terrestrial entities, cosmic fungi, and other non-Euclidean monstrosities even exist, Night Office Asset Resource Management makes no guarantee that procedures, policies, and practices as suggested in this training manual make any effort whatsoever to follow these existing guidelines, mandates, and statutes. Nor does Night Office Asset Resource Management assume any responsibility—implied, implicit, or suggested to the contrary—for psychological, physical, and/or mental damage, grief, or distress a potential candidate may incur as a result of, or during the process of, or in the aftermath of completing this training manual.

INSTRUCTIONS: This Night Office Asset Resource Managment psychological assessment exercise is a series of interwoven narrative choices that will test your mental acuity and psychological alacrity. At the end of each passage, the candidate will be provided with a variety of narrative options. It is up to them to decide which path is the correct path. Candidates should continue to explore the narrative branches until they reach an end point, where they will find a summary statement and an assessment score. At that time, the psychological assessment exercise is complete.

Candidates should refer to the Appendix of this training manual for further information regarding their assessment score. Once a candidate is satisifed with their assessment score, they should inform Night Office Asset Resource Management, who will make a summary judgement in regards to the candidate's psychological readiness for a Night Office field operative position.

SHORT FORM ACKNOWLEDGEMENT: The act of turning this page is a tacit acknowledgment on the part of the candidate that they are engaging in this psychological assessment exercise, and that they do so of their own volition.

Candidates further acknowledge that they are not being forced to undertake this assessment as a proxy agent for another individual, being, or entity that might have co-opted their intelligence.

Read & Understood: _____

[initials]

I

"You're late," Pearson says. He's waiting for you on the dark porch of the Zelphepjer estate. It is a cloudy night, and the light from the street slashes through the stark branches of the trees on the estate grounds, leaving pale marks across the front of the foreboding mansion.

Pearson has the fidgets. You can tell by the acrid cigarette haze enveloping him. He hand rolls them, using some noxious foreign tobacco. It makes you think of old tires and autopsies. The *ole auto-da-fé aroma*, as the Old Man used to call it—that hot smell of car crashes, which is totally not what the word means, but everything reminded the Old Man of death. You got used to the way he twisted things, and after he was gone, you started to understand what he was talking about.

Maybe that's what happens when you get old. There weren't many like him. There never are. Life expectancy isn't great in this business.

"Couldn't find my cat," you say.

You don't actually have a cat *per se*. You have pictures at your desk, but they are for show. It makes you seem like everyone else, and when you do slip and mention Mr. Fish—because you have, on occasion—the others automatically think you are talking about the cat in those pictures. think you are talking about the one-eyed cat in all those snapshots. In fact, you had to source those pictures from a local photographer because you said something once about how monocular vision creates physical world navigation challenges to Borlucci in Accounting, and she latched on to that like a lamprey. *He saved my life*, you finally admitted to her after the third or fourth time she pestered you. *That's why he only has one eye.*

Which is a real hand-wavy, ten-thousand-meter version of the truth, but you had already said too much and you weren't going to be able to roll it back. Therefore, you needed cover, which is why you got some pictures and made up a bunch of stories to go along with them. About how Mr. Fish likes tuna and sunshine and stupid pet shit like that.

Only the Old Man knew the truth, and he kept his side of the bargain. You knew things about him too. *It's called detente, kid,* he said when he cut the deal. It's the way the world works, deep down in the belly of the beast.

"You worry about that cat too much," Pearson says.

You ignore him.

"Where's Archer?" you ask.

He gives you a funny look. "Why are you asking about her?" he asks.

You feel your face tighten, and you try to not grimace. "Did she go around to the back?"

There's always supposed to be three operatives on a job. You're not even in the house yet, and already the team has split up.

You knew this assignment was going to be a shit job. Pearson had a reputation among the operatives, and Archer . . . well, seeing her name at the top of the rotation roster had put you in a mood.

You and Archer have some history after all, don't you?

Pearson shakes his head. "We going to do this or are you going to be fussy about her?"

"Let's do this," you say. You're not willing to let him get under your skin.

Go to 2.

"We're supposed to work together," you say.

You're not in a rush to start the job without having the Way working between the Opener and Closer. You better go check on Archer.

Go to 3.

2

The Zelphepjer House is scheduled to be knocked down next week—routine demolition as local developers continued their efforts to gentrify the North Shore. It wasn't in the Register, which means a smudger and a bagman would have been sufficient. Hell, Tooley, that fellow from the Shed who knows how to keep the vacuum hoses untangled, could probably have done it himself. Set up some fans, charcoal a bunch of sage and St. John's Wort, and let it all air out while he vacuumed.

But no, some lawyer for some great-great grandnephew or something got excited about rumors of impropriety and illicit activities—weird shit that happened one summer a long, long time ago. The lawyer filed an injunction, and everything ground to a halt. The developer didn't play nice—few of them do these days—and the judge kicked it to the County Assessor, who didn't have much choice but to call the Night Office.

You were pretty sure the dipshit lawyer was getting a good scolding from a senior partner about that injunction. *You don't get the Night Office involved,* they'd be shouting. *Not for some unverifiable crap the neighbors said fifty years ago . . .*

Anyway, the routine gets disturbed, a full sweep is scheduled, and a team gets assembled. And here you are, waiting for Pearson to put on his Hand and deal with the door.

Every Opener has their own Hand, and Pearson's is a leather contraption that looks like a tarantula attached to the back of a racing glove. The fingers fit into metal caps that have tiny spikes on the inside. When he cinches the glove tight and extends his fingers, the metal straps pull the caps against his fingertips, drawing blood.

And you can't do anything without blood, so . . .

Pearson flexes his fingers a couple of times, and you feel the familiar change in the air. The back of your left hand starts to itch—but it's been like that ever since that time upstate, when you lost a team member and got burned. You're learning how to ignore that crawling sensation.

Pearson grabs the ornate handle of the door. The door resists for a moment, but then the lock rolls over like an obedient dog. You hear the latch click, and there's a tiny *whuff* of dead air as Pearson breaks the seal on the house.

Standard field operative procedure calls for a twenty-six second wait, but Pearson starts to fidget after fourteen seconds. You wonder if he's going to be like this for the whole time.

"Clear," he says. "You ready?"

"Sure," you say. You don't bother to remind him of the count. "Let's go in."

Go to 6.

You hesitate. You are supposed to be a team of three. Where's Archer? You'd better go find her first.

Go to 5.

3

You walk widdershins around the house, following the first rule of dealing with the unknown: always keep your wards up. There's a solarium on the western side of the house, but the whole exterior has been covered with a wire mesh. Most of the window are broken, and it looks like heavy drapes have been hung inside. *At least there's some air getting into the house*, you think. It won't be totally stale, which is a relief. Spores and fungi are such a pain in the ass . . .

A large concrete patio with a covered porch spills out from the back of the house. It was fancy once, but ivy has gotten into the stonework, and the porch and columns look like they belong in an abandoned ruin. There's a railing along the edge of the roof, suggesting that there's an upper deck with access from the second floor of the house.

Behind the house, steps lead down to an area with a pool and a yard, set apart from each other by low concrete walls. There's an outbuilding as well. Looks like a utility building. Past it, the hedges start. They are wild and tangled from years of neglect. Not a good place to get lost tonight . . .

You see something moving in the pool, and when you peer over the concrete half-wall, you spot a slight figure dressed all in black. Her pale hair is drawn tight, and it hangs like a thin dagger down her back. She's investigating the bottom of the pool.

"Archer." You say her name gently so as to not spook her, but she nods like she already knows you are there.

"Come take a look at this," she says.

You go over to the edge of the pool. The bottom is filled with leaves and dirt. There's a skeleton of some animal in the shallow end. Archer is standing near the middle of the pool. She's cleared a section of detritus. It's hard to be sure in this light, but you can see marks on the ground that look too straight to be striations in the stone.

You'd prefer to keep your distance for the time being, and so you stay on the edge and ask: "What is it?"
Go to 4.

Archer looks up and sees your hesitation. "You can't see it from over there," she says. With a sigh, you drop down from the edge of the pool.
Go to 7.

4

"It's a ritual circle," Archer says. She traces the wide arc with the toe of her boot. "Looks like a copper inlay."

"Is it sealed?" you ask.

She shakes her head. "Scored in three places."

"Deep?"

"Deep enough," she says. She gives you a look—a professional look, not like the way she used to look at you when you both weren't working—and you nod back. All professional-like.

You are both on the same page here. Copper isn't that hard to score, but why do it three times when one is enough?

You look at the skeletal remains. *Too small*, you think. *Just a dog*.

A slight breeze whisks through the yard, stirring up leaves and you can't help but look over at the hedges. They appear even more ominous and twisted than they did a few minutes ago. The moon has slipped behind some clouds too.

"It's going to get colder," you say. "We should get on with the job."

"Go ahead," Archer says. "I want to look around a bit more." She kicks at the dirty bottom of the pool. "Who knows what else is under this crap."

Against your better judgment, you say, "You want some help?"

Go to 11.

"This is a team operation," you say. "And we're supposed to clear the house. Not the yard." Which is a bit pedantic, but she's not exactly sticking to the job parameters. She should know better. Keep it tight. Keep it professional. And stay on task.

Go to 13.

5

"I don't like waiting," Pearson says.

You don't either. But you shouldn't go into a job blind. "We need her eyes," you remind Pearson. "*I* need her eyes."

He's an Opener. His job is easy. You have the harder job.

Pearson doesn't say anything, but you can feel his annoyance. He's not pissed about the rules. He knows the rules get optional real quick when you're on-site. No, he's just annoyed you're in charge. Technically, speaking, the three of you are supposed to operate equally, even though your responsibilities are clearly delineated. But, it always comes down to the Closer. They're the ones who have final say. If the Closer isn't going to commit, then there's no point in proceeding . . .

However, the door's already open. You can talk about waiting all you want, but the door is open. You're going to have to go in. You just can't leave a door open like this.

"I'm done waiting," he says. He stamps his feet, punctuating his announcement. "You coming or not?"

"All right," you say. "Let's do this."
Go to 6.

"You shouldn't go alone," you say, making one last ditch effort to keep the team together.
Go to 9.

6

The door creaks theatrically when Pearson pushes it open. You can't help but roll your eyes.

There is no light inside. The moon is at the wrong angle. All you see is darkness.

Which is better than that one house in Lincoln Park where the chandelier on the second floor landing was on fire when the team crossed the threshold . . .

Pearson taps his fingers against the cooper rod he's carrying in his other hand. The metal chimes, and a filament of light appears on the tip of the rod. He taps it again, and the wisp floats free. It goes into the house, revealing an empty foyer. Bare floors. Bare walls. Nothing but old wallpaper and wainscoting.

The wisp reaches a staircase, and it sticks on the fifth stair. Its flickering light makes for thin shadows.

The house looks like it has been stripped.

Pearson steps across the threshold, and when nothing happens, you follow. You put out a hand to keep the door from swinging shut. Not that it was going to, of course. Just old habits.

You see openings to your left and right, and the hall extends past the staircase toward the back fo the house. Right beside you is a narrow door, which is probably a coat closet.

"Check that," you say to Pearson, nodding at the door.
Go to 8.

"I got this." You step over to the coat closet.
Go to 10.

7

You drop down to the bottom of the pool. The skeleton in the corner—not that pools have corners—is probably a dog. Maybe a racoon. Nothing to worry about. Archer scrapes dirt away with her heel, and you see a glint in the moonlight. "Copper inlay," she says. She's uncovered half of a circle, as well as a variety of glyphs and symbols. You recognize most of them, having had the occasion to need a Ward of protection now and again.

"Is this the only ward?" you ask. You don't have her way of looking at things, so you can't really tell with the crap in the pool.

"Maybe," she says, which isn't all that helpful. "It's weird, though. Why would you put something like this here?"

"Could this ward project to all the water in the pool?"

She frowns. "That's not how wards work," she says. She gives you a raised eyebrow, and you reply with a faint nod. Yes, you know that's not how wards work.

"But why put it here otherwise?" you say. "Unless they never bothered to fill the pool with water . . ."

"Stranger things have happened," she says.

You wait a second to see if she's going to expand on that, and she senses your hesitation. "Look—" she starts.

"It's okay," you say. "We can be adult about it, right?"

"Sure," she says.

"If we can't work together—"

"We'll be dead," she says flatly, cutting to the chase.

"Well, yeah," you acknowledge. "There's probably nothing here . . ."

She offers you a hint of a smile. "Other than you and me . . . ?"

You draw in a deep breath. It's hard to know what is the right response . . .

"Yeah," you say. "Just you and me."
Go to 12.

You want to reach out and touch her, but you know how dangerous that is. You have to stay focused. You have to get the job done.
Go to 14.

8

Pearson flexes his fingers and reaches for the doorknob on the closet. His Hand hisses lightly when he grips the knob. He's in the way, and you can't see what he sees when he opens the door, but after a second, he closes the door. "Nothing," he says.

You try not to dwell on the tingle of unease rippling down your spine. There's something about the tone of his voice that makes you think he is lying.

"Okay," you say. "Let's keep moving."
Go to 13.

"Maybe I should check it too," you say. "Just to be sure."
Go to 16.

9

Pearson shakes his head at your intractability about the rules. He shoves the door open. It's dark in the house, and he taps his fingers against the copper rod he's holding in his left hand. A blue light swells at the tip, and holding his arcane torch up, he crosses the threshold and goes into the house.

You watch his light bob around inside the house, but you can't see much of what it is illuminating. Looks like an empty foyer. Nothing but old wallpaper and wooden floors.

You glance away, looking toward the side of the house, wondering—again—where Archer is. A sudden slap of noise startles you, and you look back at the front door.

It's closed.

You rush up to the porch and try the handle on the door. It doesn't budge. You pound on the heavy panel, shouting Pearson's name. You have no idea if he can hear you, and when there isn't any response to your noise-making, you give up.

This isn't good. Pearson is the Opener, and now he's on the other side of this locked door.

You can always try to break the door down, even though it seems like it is carved from a single slab of old growth wood.
Go to 17.

Give up on this jerk and head for the back. Maybe you and Archer can figure out how to work together long enough to find another way in.
Go to 3.

10

The knob rattles a bit and the door is stiff, but you pull it open.

Only then do you realize that you've done the Opener's job for him, and, well, there's a reason everyone has a specific job on the team.

There's nothing beyond the door except darkness. In fact, it's not the inside of a closet darkness, but the void of the Abyss sort of darkness. You try to look away, but you can't help it. It is the Abyss, after all, and when you stare into it, it stares back at you. Rather, the monster there stares back.

You know what it's like to have your soul flayed apart, don't you? No, of course you don't. If you did, you would't have opened the door. But you did, and now the monster in the Abyss is tearing you apart.

You want to tell Pearson that you're sorry, but you've forgotten how to speak. You want to tell him to feed Mr. Fish, but you know Pearson won't understand what you mean. You want to fight back, but the monster has taken your will to move and to act. Your identity goes next, and then all that remains is a fading memory of sadness. Which is pretty sad, in and of itself. But even that doesn't last forever . . .

YOU ARE A CLOSER, NOT AN OPENER.
THIS IS THE WORST WAY TO DIE. SERIOUSLY.

ASSESSMENT SCORE: 0

Please refer to the Appendix for further information regarding your Assessment Score.

11

Using your shoes to clear away the dirt and leaves, you and Archer uncover two more ritual circles. The circle in the center of the pool is a large summoning circle, and the other two are filled with intricate symbols.

You parse the wards in the circle close to the wall in the shallow end. "This one is for control," you say.

"That makes this one the altar," Archer says. She's standing halfway between you and the larger circle in the deep part of the pool. "This is where they did the sacrifices."

You've seen arrangements like this before, but not out in the open. They are usually hidden in some secret chamber, away from prying eyes. Away from casual indifference. You can't accidentally switch one of these on, any more than you could accidentally transmute lead into gold, but that doesn't mean there isn't residual power in such markings. But it is strange to find them in a pool like this. The chemicals used in modern pools would react with the copper, and the last thing anyone would want is for the integrity of their magic circles to be compromised.

Archer gets that look in her eyes, and you know she's tapping into the etheric vibrations of the place. "All of this has been here for awhile," she says distantly. "Long before . . ."

Before whatever nonsense happened in the house that brought the property to the attention of the Night Office, you finish silently. It doesn't look like the recent tenants used the pool, and you can't help but wonder if they knew what had happened here.

"Were they ever successful?" you ask Archer.

She turns slowly. "Yes," she says.

A shudder runs through her body, and she takes an involutary step back from the sacrificial circle.

"No," she says. When she looks at you, she's not seeing you. "Oh, God. They made a mess of it."

Of course they did. That's why you're here.

Her gaze returns to the pool. "So much blood," she whispers.

No one ever calls the Night Office if a few Band-Aids are required.

Tell Archer to get on with it.
Go to 18.

You know better than to interrupt an operative when they are in the Way.
Go to 19.

12

After acknowledging the frisson that brought you two together in the first place, you wander off to the shallow end of the pool where you scrape leaves and dirt with your heel. Ostensibly, you're checking for more copper circles, but mostly you're taking a moment to get your heart back under control.

How did this even happen? You ask yourself. Six hours ago, you were pissed you were going to be working with her—you even went so far as to come up with a lame excuse as to why the three of you couldn't come in one car. *Couldn't find my cat,* was your excuse.

You glance back at Archer, and then look away quickly before she notices. You are going to be vulnerable, and if there is some monster here, it will try to amplify your emotional distress.

It'll be fine, you tell yourself, and then, because it doesn't sound convincing in your head, you say it out loud.

"What was that?" Archer pipes up.

"Nothing," you say. "Look, I think there's just the one circle." *Focus on the job.*

She nods. "You think Pearson is still waiting for us?" she asks, changing the subject. Almost as if she was having the same thoughts you were . . .

"I doubt it," you says. "He's an Opener. We shouldn't have left him unsupervised in front of a locked door like that. I'm going to check on him." Splitting up isn't resolving the tension between the two of you, but you are on a job.

Go to 15.

"He's got it under control," you say. "We should stick together."
Go to 20.

13

Pearson's wisp makes enough light for you to see there are two rooms off the foyer. A staircase runs up to the second floor, and tucked past it, is a narrow hall. You suspect it runs back to the kitchen.

You and Pearson listen for a minute, and hear nothing but the distant hiss of wind whispering through narrow spaces. "Not sealed up that tight," Pearson says.

You nod in agreement, and your spine unkinks a little at this realization. Things fester in places that are sealed up tight, and its never good when things fester.

"Which side do you want?" Pearson asks, indicating the two rooms off the foyer. You can't believe he's suggesting that you split up. You consider calling him on it, but you can tell he's already bored and done with this job. If you say anything, he's just going to get even more petulant with you.

What an asshole, is what you think. "Left," is what you say.
Go to 25.

What a prick, is what you think. "Right," is what you say.
Go to 26.

14

You want to reassure Archer, but you don't dare. Not now. Not when you are in the middle of a job. It's too dangerous, and so you hide your feelings away. "I'm going to check out that outbuilding," you say gruffly, pointing to the utility shed behind the pool.

Some of the light in Archer's eyes goes out, and it makes your heart ache to see that fire die, but you know it is for the best. "Okay," she says quietly. "I'll be right behind you." She offers you a brave smile. Letting you know she understands.

You still feel like shit when you climb out of the pool and head for the shed. This is exactly what you wanted to avoid. Everything was better when you both could ignore your shared history. You didn't see each other; you didn't work together. Eventually, it would all fade, and maybe you could be civil to one another.

Maybe.

The shed looks to be in better shape than the main house. It has one set of windows on the side closest to the house. Several panels of glass have been broken, and there is a board leaning against the wall inside, blocking any view. The large panel doors are mounted on rollers and move sideways, though the one on the left has come off its track. There's a chain through the handles of both doors and a heavy padlock.

This would be easier with an Opener, but it's just a padlock. Old school methods still work. You dig out your kit from one of the pockets of your jacket and get to work. The mechanism is stiff from being out in the weather this long, and you bend at least one pick before you get a good feel for the teeth. You rake them a couple of times, and the lock grudgingly opens.

You slip the chain off the right-hand door and let it dangle. Without consciously thinking, you close the lock around the last link of the chain. It's an occupational hazard of your profession. All the doors in your apartment are closed all the time too. You learn to live with the compulsion. It's what keeps you alive, after all.

Anyway, the righthand door is fussy, and you have to coax it to get it moving. The wheels screech like tortured owls as they finally shift, and then the utility shed is open.

Check out the shed.
Go to 21.

You'd better wait for Archer.
Go to 22.

15

When you get back to the front of the house, Pearson isn't on the porch. It's out of protocol for him to go on without you, but you're not surprised. He's not a very patient man, which is partly why you don't like getting paired up with him. Did he bail on this mission? *What an asshole*, you think as you wander up to the porch.

You try the door handle, just in case. It doesn't budge, and your assessment of this job continues its downward trend.

Exhaling loudly, you turn slowly and survey the yard. There's no sign of Pearson. *Great*, you think. *So much for teamwork.*

Unless . . .

You turn and look at the door again.

Did he really go in there without you?

Try to open the door the old-fashioned way, using your shoulder and/or boot.

Go to 17.

Decide both of your teammates are terrible about working with others and call it a night.

Go to 23.

16

Pearson shrugs like he doesn't care one way or another, and he steps away from the closet so you can get at it. You take hold of the knob, expecting to feel something for some reason, but it's just a metal knob. The door opens easily enough and . . .

It's an empty coat closet. Not even a wire hanger.

"Well, that was anticlimactic," you say as you close the door.

Pearson doesn't respond, and in fact, when you turn around, he's not there at all.

"Oh, great," you mutter. *What the hell is he playing at?* How did he manage to vanish like that? He didn't seem like the sort who would scamper off, much less do so quietly. And when you were working? There's no excuse for that.

"Pearson," you say loudly. "Stop messing around."

There's no response. On the stairs, Pearson's wisp gutters out, and you're suddenly in the dark, by yourself.

Fuck this, you think.
Go to 27.

This wasn't the plan, you think.
Go to 28.

17

Remember the last time you tried to break a door down? You nearly fractured an ankle, and you had bruises for weeks. This door looks really solid, and there's no way you're going to bust it open. You'd have better luck going through the plywood on one of those windows, which, now that you think about it . . .

You check the windows on the right. Whoever sealed up the house pulled off the old shutters and slapped plywood over the frames. Not the tightest seal in the world, which means there's some air flow in the old house. After a quick investigation, you find one of the frames is more rotten than the others. It doesn't take long to work the plywood loose. The nails protest, and it sounds like rats shrieking, but eventually the board comes free.

You have to scramble a bit to get up and over the windowsill. The hole isn't as big as you thought it was, but it's enough. You crawl through and slide into the darkness.

You put your back against the wall beneath the window and try to catch your breath. The moon—having gotten curious about your antics—is peering through the window. It offers enough illumination for you to see that you're in an empty sitting room. There's nothing here but dust on the floor. As your eyes adjust to the dimness, you make out two openings that lead out of this room.

You've got an LED flashlight one of your coat pockets. You get it out and click it on. Empty sitting room all right. Dust in the air. Two doors out here.

As you consider which way to go, you notice the pattern on the wallpaper. It looks like cat skulls. When you flick the light away and then back again, the pattern is more like a *fleur de lis*. *Bargain rack*, you think.

Which? Something whispers in the back of your brain. *The pattern or the hallucination?*

Your grip tightens on the flashlight. It's a little soon for reality to start stretching. You catch yourself before you start dwelling on the rumors you've heard about this house. *Don't go there,* you tell yourself.

That's how it starts. This is a routine job. There's nothing here.

Start at the front of the house, you think. *Work your way back.*
Go to 24.

If the sitting room is empty, it's likely the rest of the front part of the house is too. Might as well head to the back of the house.
Go to 25.

18

Every job has a trinity of operatives: an Opener, a Closer, and the one who sees the Way. *Think of the universe as a book*, the Old Man said on the first day of training. *There are three things you can do with it: you can open it, you can close it, and you can read its pages. That's what an on-site team is: someone who kicks down doors and break things, someone to wrap it all up and tie it off, and someone to tell you what to kick, what to break, what to leave alone, and when it's time to burn it all down and salt the earth on your way out.*

He was terrible about metaphors.

While all field operatives are taught the rudimentary skills to perform as any of the three parts of the trinity, you would eventually get assigned to the branch with which you demonstrate the most aptitude. If you showed very little ability in any of three, then it was Accounting or the Shed for you. Which isn't a death sentence, really. An organization only works as well as its infrastructure.

Anyway, the one drawback of this model is you end up with willful personalities on a team, which can make consensus difficult, especially if you are wondering if one of the others has been co-opted by a foreign intelligence. Someone who can see the Way makes it less likely that one of the others on the team will have their personality sucked out and replaced with a quivering mass of space jelly.

Of course, you can get lost in the Way too, but that's a different sort of peril.

Working for the Night Office isn't like other jobs, where the only peril is boredom. It's fairly well documented that most field operatives either go insane, die horribly, or beg for a transfer to Accounting. Of course, Accounting isn't keen on being a dumping ground for burn-outs and failures, and so they have a mandatory waiting period. Not to mention they don't post jobs openings all that often. Just because you lose a quarter of your brain to a space octopus doesn't mean Standards and Practices is going to fall all over themselves to find you a safe desk.

Most operatives leave after a season or two, bailing for something less threatening like pulling espresso shots for some not-quite-as-soul-sucking corporate giant. The job fits their newly designated mental fitness level: lots of mind-numbing repetition, weekends off, overtime pay during holidays, and a brain full of banal pop music that's been programmed by the central office to be as bland as the house blend.

"Hey, Archer, you going to come back this way soon?"

Man, introspection sucks when you're on the job. Always so dark and cynical.

When she looks at you again, you know she's back because she's totally giving you that death stare. Which is good. Slightly pissed off operatives are always better than distracted operatives. You smile and give her a "let's wrap this up" wave.

"They killed goats here," she says. "Little baby ones."

"Of course they did," you say. Humanity rarely surprises you anymore.

"What did they summon?" you ask. "And what happened to it?" you add, recalling the gashes in the copper circle that was supposed to keep eldritch horrors in place.

She raises an arm and points toward the house. On cue, you hear someone yelling, and it sounds like it's coming from inside the house.

"Pearson opened the door," you say. "He didn't wait for us."

Race around to the front of the house.
Go to 30.

Grab Archer and head for the back of the house. The most direct route is the best route.
Go to 31.

19

There are always three on an job: an Opener, a Closer, and the third—the one who sees the Way. It's all more complicated than that, obviously, but the names are from before the Old Man's time. *Sometimes we stick with the old ways because they're simple and they work*, is what he used to say.

The Opener is the one who clears the path. They're the ones who are most sought after by the opposition, because if they can be co-opted, they can facilitate the invasion. The Closer is their opposite. They are the ones who shut things down. Who set the world right. They are the badasses the other side wants dead, because they're the ones who can send them all scurrying back to whatever empty void they're trying to catapult out of.

That leaves the Way, and these operatives are the seers, the psychics, the witchy men and women. They see beyond the possible into the statistical variances of the improbable, the impossible, and the inexplicable. Moreover, looking creates a connection. If they look too hard, they might see something they don't want to see.

Look, the future is no more fixed than the past, which is to say that the act of looking at it is what changes it from possibility mixed with probability into something fixed and rushing headlong at you.

The Way to Heaven is paved with Good Intentions, the old saying goes. *The Way to Hell is cobbled with the bones of those who looked too far*, is another saying. One that doesn't get as much time as it should.

Our craving for narrative can—literally—change the Universe. You'd think we'd be better custodians of this power.

Anyway, it's best to not rush a seer when they are telescoping the past. Dialing in at the right depth is a tricky business, and the last thing you need is someone pestering you to hurry it up.

You climb out of the pool and wander over to the utility shed. It's a squat building with all the appeal of a dirty brick. The single window on the side facing the house has been boarded over, and its doors are warped panels that are mounted on metal rails. A length of chain runs through the handles, and it is fastened with a rusty padlock.

You could fuss with the lock, but the chain is easier. You get out the bolt cutters from your jacket. It takes a minute or two to cut a link, but in the end, the chain comes off.

Open the shed.
Go to 21.

Wait for Archer before you go into the shed.
Go to 22.

20

You survey the rest of the yard, eyeing the tangled hedges in the back as well as the dilapidated building near the pool. It has a set of large doors on rollers, and a single window that has been boarded over. There are shadows everywhere since the moon is being coy with the clouds. The wind slithers along your collar and tickles your neck.

In most cases, the confluence of bad mojo is in the house itself, and a Closer's job is more easily done at the point of greatest psychic intensity. Rarely do you see much activity in the surrounding property.

Though, to be fair, this is the first time you've run into a magic circle laid into the bottom of a pool. Clearly, there was ritual activity outside the house. This place might be an exception to the rule.

"Let's start with that shed," you say.
Go to 35.

"I want to check out the maze," Archer says. She seems like she has the scent of something.
Got to 37.

21

The outbuilding is a combination utility shop, garden shed, and storage for pool equipment. There are dusty shelves, a work table, and a tiny alcove at the back where there was a toilet and sink. An old poster of a sandy beach is still attached to one of the walls. It looks like it had been glued in place, though it has faded so much that the beach is almost translucent.

There's nothing in the room that suggests an infection of cosmic horrors. Well, except for some tiny mushrooms growing in a fuzzy mound in one corner, but that's pretty normal for an abandoned work shack that used to store chemicals and garden implements.

After a fruitless search, you leave the shed. Archer is still in the pool. She's wandering around like she has lost a contact lens or she's listening intently to the phantom gurgles of the water filtration system that has long since rotted out.

She's going to be at it for awhile, you think. You might as well head back to the front of the house.

Go to 15.

God, these two are a pain in the ass to work with. They're trying to justify being called out. There's nothing here.

Go to 23.

22

You wave Archer over, and she joins you at the open door of the shed. "You want to look first?" you ask.

She nods, and her face tightens as she peers into the Way.

There's a very technical term for that place where psychics go, and the operations manual for how to navigate the Way without losing your mind runs to eighteen volumes. Each one is thicker than your fist. There are only three copies of the manual—none of this information is digitized, naturally—and access is highly restricted. The Ops Desk has one copy in the ward room; there's a second in the Library; and the third used to be with the Old Man, but his successor redecorated the offices and no one's seen the copy since.

Anyway, every operator get time with the Books of the Way as part of their training, and obviously those who are cosy with slipping in and out of the Way get more access than the rest of the trainees. You never showed much inclination to surf past the warning markers of the psyche, which means that a lot of the witchy stuff is beyond you. It's okay; they profess the same wonder and amazement about how many pockets you have in your jacket.

That's just good tailoring, frankly.

At a very rudimentary level, you know Archer can see in the dark. You could too, probably, if you bothered to practice, but there's a part of you that likes the shadows. You don't need to see everything all the time. The human brain can't process all of that sensory input anyway. It's just going to make you pay attention less. It's like being in a room with really bright lights. You end up squinting, which narrows your field of vision as well as your attention span.

Archer's head moves slowly as she scans the dark interior of the shed. "They used to store gardening supplies in here." She lifts her hand and points at an indeterminate spot. "There was a little greenhouse there."

"Anything make your skin crawl?" you ask.

"There is blood," she says.
Go to 33.

"I . . . I hear someone crying," she says.
"Well, that certainly qualifies," you say.
Go to 34.

23

You return to your car. As you drive away from the Zelphep-jer House, you start considering how you're going to write your report. Insubordination and indiscretion of other members of the team? A team that doesn't think together doesn't cohere, and non-coherence is bad. It was one of the first lessons the Old Man hammered into you. *You can't be the only one paying attention*, he said. *One set of eyes isn't enough.*

Of course, that's if the others file any sort of grievance against you in their reports. If it turns out that it was nothing but an old house, filled with stale air and decaying whispers, then you weren't needed. Why bring a Closer if there's nothing to close? Sure, they'll be grumpy that you bailed on them, but it's not like anyone was in any real danger.

By the time you park your car under your apartment building, you've convinced yourself there wasn't anything there. It was just an old house that some great-great-great-grandnephew was a snit about it being torn down. No one likes having their history wiped out of existence, but it happens all the time. *Nothing is built to last anymore*, you think as you pass the still out-of-order elevator in the lobby of the building.

You climb the stairs to your fourth floor apartment. It's in the southwest corner, and it looks out over the cemetary. *They were supposed to plant trees*, the landlord said when he saw you noticing the view. *But there were budget cuts or something.*

He got nervous after that, thinking you weren't going to rent the place. Judging from the way he fidgeted, he's been having trouble with getting someone to take this unit. You made some noise about how you might be able to make it all work, except that, you know . . . He got the hint and eagerly offered a discount on the rent. But only if you signed a lease.

You pretended to think it over a bit before you agreed.

They still haven't put in the trees yet.
You don't mind. The view suits you.
Mr. Fish likes it too.

THIS IS A DISAPPOINTING ENDING.
IT DISPLAYS A LACK OF TEAM SPIRIT, AS WELL AS AN
INSULAR MIND THAT PREFERS THE COMPANY OF DEAD
THINGS.

ASSESSMENT SCORE: N/A
PLEASE SEE THE PROCTOR.

Please refer to the Appendix for further information regarding your Assessment Score.

24

The foyer would be large enough to turn an elephant around in, if it weren't for the thick bannister of the grand staircase that goes up to the second floor. You play the beam of your flashlight around. There's another room on your left, and there is a hall beside the staircase that leads to the back of the house. Probably where you'll find the kitchen and maybe a couple other rooms.

The walls are covered with old wallpaper, and the rectangular spots suggest that framed pictures once hung on it in various places. There's a layer of dust on the floor which is helpful because you can see Pearson's tracks.

He came in, turned around once, and then went right on down that side hall, toward the back of the house.

You shine the light down the hall. There's a door at the back, and it's closed. *Of course it is*, you think.

You run the light across Pearson's tracks again. *At least he came in*, you think. He didn't run off and leave you.

There's not much else to see in the foyer. You try the front door, and are not surprised to find that it is stuck shut. It's not locked—you flip the lock back and forth a few times—it's just not going to open.

This house is starting to annoy you.

Cross the foyer to the room on the opposite side.
Go to 39.

Follow Pearson's footprints.
Go to 41.

25

There was probably a chandelier of some kind in the dining area. Judging from the way the wallpaper has faded, there was probably also a large hutch or sideboard along the far wall. You pace off the room, and figure there's enough space for a table that could sit a dozen or so.

Other than that, the room is empty. There's not even a mysterious stain on the floor. This might be the least threatening room in the whole place.

You dawdle for a minute. This might be your last chance. You should probably make sure everything is copacetic, including your heartrate.

Head back to the foyer.
Go to 24.

That archway at the back of the room probably leads to the kitchen.
Go to 40.

26

You take out a small flashlight from one of the many secret pockets in your jacket. Turning it on, you go to the right and check out the empty sitting room. There's no furniture here, and the windows are all boarded over. A open doorway at the back of the room probably leads to the kitchen. The wallpaper is as dull as the stuff in the hall, and you play your flashlight beam across a couple of water stains on the ceiling, but nothing seems out of the ordinary.

Well, *ordinary* is relative, of course. You are, after all, investigating a supposedly haunted house.

Since there isn't much to see, you head for the opening at the other end of the room, where you find a dining room that is as empty as the sitting room. Except for the spider building a web in the corner of the ceiling. When you shine your light on it, it scuttles into a tiny crack.

You don't blame it. You can come off as a scary monster.

Since there is nothing here either, you might as well continue on to the kitchen, which is probably the room through the arch at the back of the dining room.

Go to 42.

Return to the foyer.
Go to 44.

27

There's a time for pranks, and there's a time for saving your own skin. *If you want to fight the horror on your own, you'll have better luck trying to stop a speeding bus with your forehead*, the Old Man liked to say. You're not about to take on whatever is hiding in this house by yourself. If it turns out the others on your team are having a laugh at your expense, well, whatever. You didn't like them either.

As you turn for the exit, you pride yourself on having been smart enough to block the door open, and then you remember you didn't.

It slams shut, almost as if whatever malevolence there is in the house wanted to give you one last glimpse of freedom before yanking it away.

Behind you, something shuffles in the hall. You don't think it is Pearson.

"Oh, you wanna play?" You unbutton your jacket and turn around.

Go to 36.

No, seriously. Fuck. This.
Go to 38.

28

You're not going to panic. Panic is what kills. Panic is what breeds monsters. You didn't get to be a Closer by panicking.

You retrieve the powerful flashlight from one of the many inner pockets of your jacket. Unlike Pearson, you prefer modern tools. As long as you check the batteries regularly, these tools tend to work. Clicking on the light, you examine the foyer. It's empty, and the wallpaper is six kinds of drab.

The hall stretches back beyond the staircase, and it looks like it leads to a kitchen and probably another room at the back of the house. On your left is a room that looks like it used to be a library; on your right is a formal sitting room, though there's nothing formal or comfortable about it now.

There's no sign of Pearson. It's like he wasn't ever here.

You wander over to the stairs and shine the light up. There's a landing up there. Along with more rooms. When you bring your light back down, you notice a tiny alcove under the stairs. *A bounty of choices*, you think, trying to sound calm. Meanwhile, the Old Man is waving his arms in your head. *Where the fuck is your partner? Why'd he ditch you?*

The front door slams shut with such force that the whole house rattles.

You turn slowly, letting your light play over the closed door.

Keep your wits about you. You're a professional.
Go to 50.

Now is as good a time as any to lose your shit.
Go to 52.

29

The room off the foyer used to be a library, and most of the walls are covered with built-in bookcases. The shelves have been swept clean a long time ago, and you don't find much except for a few moldering gothic romances. One of them features a pulpy cover of a woman in a flimsy nightgown, fleeing in terror from a hooded figure with glowing eyes.

There's an inscription on the inside of the cover.

"To E, Remember this night? —B"

You wonder if E is the woman in the sheer nightgown. She probably doesn't recall the evening in exactly the same way. You're about to put the book back on the shelf when you realize the house in the background is *this* house, though the surrounding landscape is all wrong.

With a grimace, you put the book back, recognizing the early symptoms of what the Old Man used to call Gothic Myopia— when you're so caught up in an investigation that you start imagining more symbolic representation than is actually there. Coincidences start piling up. Shadows get deeper. When it gets really bad, you start seeing monsters that aren't there. If you stay too long in the heightened state all operatives work in, the world really does start to warp around you.

You're surprised it's coming on so quickly. Usually it takes a few hours before your visual field smears like this.

It's time to check in with Pearson.
Go to 45.

This is just a little work-related stress. It's nothing. You're fine.
Got to 49.

30

You and Archer race around to the front of the house, where the front door gapes open ominously. *Thank God, it wasn't one of those possessed houses that slams doors*, you think as you dash through the front door. Archer is right behind you.

And that's when the door slams shut behind you.

"Are you fucking kidding me?" you explode.

Before you can complain any further, Archer grabs your arm and points into the room on the left side of the dusty foyer.

There's a roaring fire burning in the hearth, and its ruddy light illuminates a room full of empty bookcases. It's hard to tell what color the bookcases and floor are supposed to be, what with the firelight, the shadows, and all that blood.

"So much blood," Archer whispers, her hand tight on your arm.

Someone—you suspect Pearson—has been dismembered in a horrific fashion, and the room has been painted with his blood. There are chunks of him everywhere, and daintily nibbling on pieces are—

"Baby goats," Archer whimpers.

In any other circumstances, you'd go "Aww, aren't they cute?," because they are, but they're snacking on human flesh and none of the gore in the room is sticking to their fur. It's not because they're spectral goats or they've been sprayed with a stain guard or something. It's because they're—

You look away.

They're grooming each other. With their tongues.

Archer makes a noise like she is going to vomit, and you don't blame her. You might do the same yourself, except that you know it's all an illusion.

It fits too perfectly with what you were just talking about. Blood sacrifices. Baby goats. Something dark and foreboding being released into this world.

"Get ahold of yourself, Archer," you say. "It's feeding on our fear."

"What?"

You snap your fingers at the goats. "Look at them. So tiny and perfect. Where did they come from? And who taught them to like human flesh? They're not real goats. They're—I dunno—a couple dozen offspring from The Black Goat of the Woods With a Thousand Young, or some other relic from the old files."

One of the goats is staring at you. It bleats unhappily when you refuse to say the real name of its mother. You quickly execute the sweeping hand gestures that zip up a corner of reality around the four-legged demon spawn.

The goat bleats once more, a warbling cry echoed by all of the others, and then they vanish like soap bubbles popping when the first one is squeezed into non-existence. Which isn't hard because they are nothing more than phantasmal illusions that you and Archer are sharing.

"We've got to keep it together up here," you say, tapping your forehead.

Go to 32.

"We've got to be strong in here," you say, putting your hand on your heart.

Go to 53.

31

You grab Archer's arm, and immediately regret doing so. She's still in the Way, and you are sucked in with her. The landscape shifts through the color spectrum—all the dark colors bleed orange and yellow, the moonlight turns gold, and the copper in the bottom of the pool turns into writhing black snakes.

The house is lit up bright and electric, as if it is made from stacks of aquamarine ice cubes. Violet energies pulse within it, and all the windows and doors ooze with white pus. There are dark things wiggling inside, like mice or ants or tiny viruses with fangs. Something shiny and red squirms in the belly of the houses and you figure it's Pearson, who hasn't made it much farther than the foyer of the house.

As you watch—your hand fixed to Archer's arm—the black biters swarm Pearson, and each one tears off a piece. There are hundreds of them, and they swarm him until there is only a black mound. When they disperse, the shiny and red figure is gone.

Archer falls to her knees, breaking the connection between the two of you. She dry heaves, and you feel like you're going to be sick yourself.

"Close it," she whispers. She flaps a hand at the magic circle in the shallow end of the pool. "They made a sacrifice. You can tap it here."

She's right. Pearson is scattered throughout the house. That's all you need. You stagger over to the magic circle, and use your hands to clear off the dirt and leaves. The copper gleams like wet blood in the moonlight. You're seeing phantom images from having fallen into the Way with Archer. They avoid the circle, whcih means it hasn't been compromised. It still works!

You crawl into the circle and get out your ceremonial knife. A bit of blood is all you need, and you travel with a ready supply of that. You stab your finger and squeeze out a few drops. As soon as your blood hits the copper, the wire starts to hum.

Yes, you think, *this will do just fine.*

Pearson's death won't be for naught . . .

THIS IS A FUNCTIONAL ENDING.
VERY BRIEF, THOUGH. IT'S BARELY ENOUGH TO ASSESS YOUR POTENTIAL, BUT YOU WON'T GET PENALIZED. THIS TIME.

ASSESSMENT SCORE: 70

Please refer to the Appendix for further information regarding your Assessment Score.

32

Wary of anything else that seems wildly out of the norm, you and Archer press on with your investigation of the house. There's a sitting room and dining area off to the right, and in the back, there's a kitchen that has been stripped of its appliances. The countertops are gone too, as are the outlet covers. In several places, the walls have been ripped out, where tweakers have come after the copper wires in the wall.

"Wait," Archer says. She's looking at the empty space beside one of the torn-up counters. "There used to be a refrigerator here."

There's an empty outlet box on the wall. "Okay," you say. "What about it?"

She frowns. "You're opening it, and there's—there's something inside."

"I'm not opening it," you say, "because there is no fridge here. You're seeing another reality."

She looks at me, her eyes wide. "Don't open the refrigerator," she whispers.

"Okay," you say. "I won't."

Her eyes narrow and her gaze turns inward. "No, it's not this refrigerator . . ." Her hand reaches for your arm, but you keep your distance. You know better than to have contact when the Way is open. "It's somewhere else. What have you—"

"Fantastic," you say, cutting her off. "So, somewhere, sometime, I'm going to open a refrigerator. That's great, Archer. And what am I going to find?" Part of you doesn't want her to answer, because it will force you to look at something you don't want to look at.

"Death," she hisses.

And there it is.

"I fucking hate working with psychics," you grumble.

You inspect the rest of the kitchen. The windows along the back wall are all boarded over, and the French doors that lead to the veranda have been blocked off with a 'x' of 2 by 4s. There's a pantry over in the corner, and in the floor, there's a wooden trapdoor. Probably leads to a cellar.

The door looks like it hasn't been opened in a long time. You use your Sharpie pen to write a series of warnings and seals along the edge of the hatch, making sure it never gets opened again.

When you turn around, Archer has vanished.

"Archer?" There's no response. Where has she gone?
Go to 54.

You don't panic. It's just an illusion, right? You are confident she is still in the room.
Go to 56.

33

"Of course there is blood," you say. There's always blood.

Archer is drawn into the shed by the power of her vision. As she drifts toward the back, you take out your flashlight and switch it on.

There's a workbench along one wall. A row of shelves form an 'L' in a corner of the room. There's a tiny bathroom in the other corner. An empty hearth in the back is framed by the end of a stove pipe hanging morosely from the ceiling.

"Here," Archer says, pointing at what seems like a random spot.

You shine the flashlight on the floor, and sure enough, there's a faded stain that looks like someone lost a few pints of blood. The edge of the stain is distinct—it's almost a straight line.

You kneel to get a closer look. "Some kind of door," you say.

Archer is distracted by something on the wall over the workbench. You swing your light around and illuminate a piece of wood. It's a face of a shaggy giant with elongated ears, fire in its eyes, and a forked tongue. "What is that?" you ask. It doesn't look like any mythological or esoteric entity you know.

Archer goes over to the mask and puls on the tongue. It moves in her hand, and you feel something shift under the floor. A gap appears, right along the line you noticed. It's a trapdoor, and you get your fingers under it and lift it all the way open.

You shine your light down into the hole. It's only a few meters deep, and there's a wooden ladder attached to the side.

"Should we investigate?"
Go to 59.

"I don't like the looks of this. We should be careful."
Go to 66.

34

"Someone's crying?" You reach for your flashlight. "In the shed?"

Archer lifts her arm. "There," she says, pointing at the tangled hedges at the back of the property.

"I don't hear anything," you say. Archer is reacting to something in the Way. Past, future, alternate possibility not yet realized: it could be any one of them. But it's enough of a signal to draw Archer's attention.

Archer shrugs, all the acknowledgment you're going to get that she's listening outside of this time and place.

"All right," you say. There's no point in arguing with her when she's like this. "Let's go check out the hedges."

You suspect you're going to find a rocky cairn—a reminder of a lost child buried long ago—but when you reach the hedges, you realize they are more extensive than you first thought. In fact, it looks like there's a whole maze back here. Who knows if it is even walkable anymore . . .

"Do you still hear it?" you ask Archer.

She shakes her head. "It was a ghost," she says. "I don't know of what, but there's something here."

You look at the choices you have of paths through the hedges. "Should we split up?"

"No!" Archer's tone brooks no discussion. "We stay together."

"That's fine with me," you say. "Which way?"

"Left," Archer says.
Go to 58.

"Right," Archer says.
Go to 60.

35

The shed is locked with a heavy chain and padlock. You may not be certified as an Opener, but that doesn't mean you don't know how to pick a lock. Archer pretends not to watch as you work your pick and rake on the old lock, though she does glance at her watch when you tug the lock open. "Less than a minute," she says.

"I don't get to practice as much as I used to," you say. You thread the chain out of the doors, and with a grunt, heave one of the doors along its track.

A draft of fetid air blasts of the shed, and you tuck your nose into your sleeve. The smell of whatever died in there has been lingering a long time. You click on your flashlight and wave it around.

It's a utility shop / garden shed. There's a work bench and pegboard for tools, and shelves run along the wall past the bench. In the back, there's a tiny alcove with a toilet and sink.

However, the altar and shrine along the back wall totally spoil the utilitarian aesthetic.

The altar is a low counter covered with a ragged cloth. A number of stuffed heads hang on the wall around it. Their creepy glass eyes glint in the flashlight's beam, and their expressions range from howls of rage to what looks like cries for help.

"Well, that's something you don't see very often," Archer says.

You give her a look. What sort of places does she frequent if she's labeling these stuffed heads as something she sees "not very often"? She acknowledges your sidelong glance with a shrug, and walks into the shed before you can ask an impertinent question.

There are two deer, one antelope, a wild boar, and three different species of cat on the wall. And one . . .

"Is that a black goat of Uhr?" you ask, pointing at the shaggy head mounted in the middle of the display. Right over the altar.

Archer nods. "I think so."

They were domesticated during the Eneolithic period, but vanished from the record during the 3rd millennium BCE. The archeological record isn't clear why, though certain fringe elements in the esoteric world claim they were related to the spawn of Shub-Niggurath, one of the numerous Great Old Ones that were all over the pages of early twentieth-century pulp horror.

Of course, the Night Office knows otherwise, which is why it is disconcerting to find a stuffed head like this on the wall in an otherwise unremarkable garden shed. They weren't wiped out five thousand years ago; they were merely wiped out *on* this planet. They're still out there.

"Is that what they summoned?" you ask Archer.

"They're trophies," she muses as she drifts toward the shrine of dead animals. "They're not trying to strike a deal with the Old Ones; they're hunting them."

"Cool," you say. It is a bit refreshing to find a site where the focus on using the arcane isn't about gaining power or having sex with an octopus, but rather, something not unlike what the Night Office is charged with: the eradication of all threats to human life, be they local or cosmic.

Go to 57.

You shake your head. Archer might be on to something, but you can't help but think the placement of the black goat has more meaning. It's too central. Like it is to be worshipped, and not merely as a prize trophy.

Go to 55.

36

The monster lunges for you, and your hand closes over the slippery five-pointed shape in the upper left pocket of your coat. You pull the stone free as the monster's jaws close around your shoulder. By the petrified testicles of St. Eramus, that hurts! Its teeth grind against your collarbone, and its fetid breath makes you choke.

You jam the stone against the side of its head, right below, uh, how many eyes does this thing have? There's no time to count them. You thumb the stone hard against its slick flesh, and whatever pain you are feeling is minor compared to what spikes through its elementary nervous system from the touch of the Elder Sign.

It growls, unwilling to let go, and its jaw tightens. Its flesh is bubbling and frothing from contact with the stone, and you slide the piece of worn soapstone across the monster's hot skin. It's like the proverbial hot knife through butter. Something pops beneath your hand, and you suspect you've just run the stone across one of the monster's eyes.

It shakes its head, which, unfortunately, means shaking you too. Your world is turned sideways, and you lose your grip on the Elder Sign. The monster slams you into the wall, driving the air out of your lungs. You gasp in pain and fear.

Where's the stone? You know it glows when it is activated. It should be here somewhere.

The monster lets go of you, and you slump to the floor, which is good because that's where the stone is, right?

You spot it over there, near the base of the stairs, and as the monster thrashes about, banging against the door and the wall, you slither across the floor. Your shoulder is on fire, and you don't think your right hand is going to work, and so you reach out with your left. It's right there! Glowing so bright.

The monster snorts. It huffs. It's coming for you again.

You grab the stone and roll onto your back.

The monster looms over you. One of its massive feet come down on your leg, and something snaps in your kneecap. It opens its jaws as it bends down, and you shove your arm into its mouth.

Its jaws close with a snap, and the pain is so intense you lose track of yourself.

When you come back, you're on the floor, shoved up against the base of the stairs. You can feel your right arm, burning like it's being devoured by a thousand fire ants. You don't feel anything on the left, because your brain has severed all connection with the pain receptors over there.

The floor is hot and slippery, and you know it's from all the blood pumping out of the ruined stump of your arm.

The monster is nearby, snarling and snapping at something it can't reach. It swallowed your arm—what a greedy bastard—and it's starting to figure out what you were holding in your fist. What is now burning like a white hot star in its belly.

The Elder Sign.

You struggle to draw enough breath to laugh. You're not the only one going to Hell tonight.

Whatever it takes, you think.

A Closer does whatever it takes . . .

YOUR HEART WAS IN THE RIGHT PLACE, BUT THIS ISN'T QUITE WHAT WE HAD IN MIND.

ASSESSMENT SCORE: 64

Please refer to the Appendix for further information regarding your Assessment Score.

37

The hedges are more than two meters tall and very dense. You don't image you could squeeze through them if you tried. Archer, though, finds a gap—almost as if she knew it was there.

When you look through the gap, you see another hedge row. You both squeeze through and stand in a narrow lane between two hedges.

Definitely a hedge maze.

"Left or right," you say to Archer.

"We shouldn't split up," she says. "That's going to end badly for both of us."

"Noted," you say. "Okay, pick a direction and let's get started."

"Left," Archer says.
Go to 58.

"Right," Archer says.
Go to 60.

38

It's embarrassing how badly you panic. After all you've gone through, this is how it ends? Mewing and shrieking and trying to claw your way through a solid core door?

Whatever is in the hall with you starts to growl and chuckle, which only increases your panic. Part of your brain is sounding like the Old Man—yelling at you to get your shit together. *Turn and fight this thing! You're a goddamned Closer. Extra-dimensional monsters are like breakfast cereal.* But his voice is lost beneath the rasping cough that fills the foyer.

Hot breath washes over you. It stinks of carrion.

You stop trying to get out. The Old Man throws you a salute and then vanishes. He's not one to go down with a doomed ship.

You turn around and put your back to the door. *Might as well face it*, you think. *Don't let it gorge on your fear.*

You can only make out a vague shape in the dark. A suggestion of a massive head. A mouth, filled with too many teeth. Wings, perhaps. Or maybe its arms are just that long . . .

Talons scrape against the floor, and in that last moment, your thoughts turn to Mr. Fish. *Who is going to take—*

WHO, INDEED?
A DISAPPOINTING EFFORT.

ASSESSMENT SCORE: 12

Please refer to the Appendix for further information regarding your Assessment Score.

39

The room on the left side of the foyer was once a library. In the back of the room, there is a raised hearth with a brick mantel. An old frame is still mounted on the wall over the fireplace, but whatever picture was in the frame has long been taken. Built-in bookcases fill three of the walls, and more bookcases flank the boarded over windows.

There are a few moldering paperbacks left on a shelf. Nothing terribly interesting. Well, a couple of gothic romances and an old French-English dictionary. You suppose it paints a quaint picture of a reader, but it's hardly in keeping with the vibe of the rest of the house.

There's a faded postcard in the dictionary. It shows a gothic castle lit with lots of torches. On the back, someone has written *"Wish you were here, —B."* The postmark is sixty years old, and the card is addressed to Miss Eliza Zelphepjer.

You didn't bother to read through all of the background notes on the house, and so you're not entirely sure who Miss Eliza was, but clearly she was missed by someone.

On the dictionary page where the card was tucked, one of the French words has been heavily underlined.

Tuerie.

Massacre.

Oh, man. Sixty-year old emo teenager drama is a drag. Get on with clearing the house already.

Go to 62.

You're got a bad feeling about this.

Go to 63.

40

The kitchen takes up the back end of the house, like all decent kitchens do. It's been stripped of its counter tops and most of its appliances. Oddly enough, there's a refrigerator here—a tall, stainless steel one that's out of place in this dismal setting.

Even stranger, it appears to have power. You can hear it humming quietly. You thought the power was off in the whole building. How is this still running?

Oh, you know a trap when you see one.
Go to 43.

Hang on. You are kinda really, *really* curious about the refrigerator.
Go to 46.

41

The alcove under the stairs used to be a water closet, but there is nothing left now but a hole in the floor and a pair of pipes jutting out of the wall. There are marks in the dust that might be footprints, but they could as easily be random patterns in the dust. Hard to tell what's really there and what you want to see, frankly. Best to not try to read too much into it.

Squeezing into the alcove, you shine the light down the hole in the floor. Something glints weakly, and you can't decide if it is just a film of long-standing water or something metallic. Either way, the hole is only a few inches wide. Your arm will get stuck, and besides, this was probably where all the shit goes when someone flushed the toilet. Whatever is down there can stay down there.

You play the light across the hole again. The glint is mocking you for being too afraid to reach for it.

I'm not, you think.

You whip the flashlight up and shine the light across the walls. You thought you heard something, but nothing is there.

When you shine the light on the hole again, nothing reflects. It's just a hole.

God damn it, you think. A trickle of sweat works its way down your back.

Return to the foyer.
Go to 62.

Check out the kitchen.
Go to 40.

Follow the hall past the kitchen.
Go to 67.

42

You and Pearson enter the kitchen, which is a narrow room that runs across the back of the house. He lobs a couple of wisps around the room, painting everything with a soft bluish glow. Large picture windows are boarded over, as are a set of French doors that would have opened to the veranda. The countertops are gone, and there are holes in the walls where tweakers have pulled the copper wire out.

It's desolate and bare, and makes you—

"Hey, what the fuck is this?"

Pearson is standing by a large stainless steel refrigerator, which appears to be receiving power. It's modern, one of those fancy sub-zero models with two doors up and a freezer compartment down below. It also has a dispenser slot where you can get filtered water and ice cubes in perfectly square shapes.

A sure sign of demonic engineering. Ice doesn't like being forced into rudimentary geometric shapes.

Pearson flexes his Hand, and his jaw flexes when the metal tips draw blood from his fingers. "You ready?" he asks.

When you nod, he presses his Hand flat on the right-hand panel of the refrigerator. The display panel above the dispenser lights up with orange ideograms. A smell of burned animal hair fills the room. When he peels his Hand off, the black handprint of his intent fades slowly.

You start counting in your head. You've only gotten to 'eight' when Pearson slaps the refrigerator again. The display panel flashes green this time, and there's no smell of burning hair.

He reaches for the handle. "Hold on," you say. "Do the full count." *He's so fucking eager for mayhem.*

He throws you a look, which you don't let under your skin. Openers are always cowboys. Closers are sticklers. That's what keeps everyone alive.

A single cube of ice falls out of the dispenser.

"Good thing I waited," Pearson says. He makes no effort to keep the note of derision out of his voice.

When he bends over to pick up the ice cube, the freezer drawer slams open. He's knocked backward, and he fetches up against the cabinets on the other side of the kitchen.

Something dark and shapeless—with too many eyes and too many tentacles—comes flying out of the freezer.

Fucking shoggoths, is the thought that flits across your brain.

Pearson's smart enough to keep his mouth shut—too many operatives yell or scream when they're attacked, and all that does is give these eldritch jellies an easy way in. He grabs a tentacle with his Hand and gives it a pulse of Opener magic.

Shoggoths don't like being Opened. Fundamentally—and functionally—they're protoplasmic blank slates. They do what you tell them to do, and they'll do it forever, which makes them excellent booby traps. Sure, there are stories about them achieving some level of low-grade animal intelligence, but after a couple million years of doing the same thing over and over, you'd probably get bored too.

But when you take something that operates on a very specific instruction set, and basically tell it to "let go," it unravels. In the case of ectoplasmic space goo, they—literally—turn to something not dissimilar to paraffin. Stiff jelly, as it were.

And if you can get deep enough in their physical mass, that root level command can do a lot of damage.

Give Pearson a hand (which is the responsible thing to do, even though he'll be an asshole about it later).

Go to 73.

Pearson can handle the shoggoth on his own (and frankly, he's the sort who'll be pissed if you actually help him, regardless of protocol).

Go to 70.

43

There's nothing else in the kitchen, except for the refrigerator which shouldn't be here. Wisely, you give it space while you investigate the rest of the room. There's a empty pantry, which is where you find a breaker panel.

All the breakers are switched off, except for one marked "kitchen storage."

You eye the refrigerator again.

Supposedly, the power has been shut off at the curb, but it wouldn't be the first time the power company didn't follow through. Someone is keeping their secret stash cold.

You take out the roll of magic tape you keep handy and return to the refrigerator. You tear off four strips, and use two on the refrigerated half and two on the freezer. You activate the magic in the tape, and it glows orange. A familiar smell of sulphur and sandalwood fills the room. You write Words of Closure on the stainless steel—Sharpies are one of the secret tools of the occult world in this modern age—and then inscribe a Ward of Sealing.

Satisfied with your work, you return to the breaker panel and flip the switch marked "kitchen storage." Nothing happens at first, but you are patient. A few minutes pass, and then you hear a faint pounding noise.

Whatever is inside the refrigerator knows the power is off, and it wants out.

Not going to happen, fridge freak, you think. You're a professional. Those doors are permanently shut.

It's time to check out the study.
Go to 67.

Wait. There's something in the main hall you missed.
Go to 41.

44

When you return to the foyer, Pearson's already there, and he looks bored. "Not much," he says when you ask him about what he found in his search. "Place has been cleaned out."

You're not as convinced, but how much of that feeling is mere annoyance at having been called out of bed for what might be a empty vessel? There's always something for an Opener to do, but quite often there's not much call for a Closer. Which is good in the long run, right? But still, it makes for not a whole lot of job satisfaction.

People who like being Closers don't last long, the Old Man used to say. *If you find joy in what you do, you're giving them a way in.*

Them being the very entities that you are supposed to be banishing.

"What's left?" you ask, shoving aside those thoughts.

"Kitchen's in the back," Pearson says.
Go to 42.

Pearson points at the stairs with his copper wand. "Upstairs," he says.
Go to 68.

45

You find Pearson under the stairs. He's hunched over, tucked into an alcove that was probably a water closet. There's a hole in the floor, and he's staring intently down at it.

"What's up?" you ask.

He stirs, as if he had been lost in thought. "Nothing," he says. He waves his gloved hand at the floor. "Just thought I saw something."

"Yeah, I'm getting that feeling too," you say. "There's something here."

"I know," he says. "I've been wanting to scratch under my balls since we came in."

"Scratch what?"

"You know. That itch you get when—you don't get that?"

"No," you say. "I don't get that."

"Huh," he says. He shrugs. "Well, I get it. Right down there. It gets worse the more bad shit there is."

You shake your head. "And, uh, how bad is it now?" You can't believe you're having this conversation with him.

"Nagging," he says. He adjusts the crotch of his trousers, and you look away. "Not bad yet. But definitely there."

"Let's keep moving," you say. "Get this over with."

"Kitchen's back there," he says, pointing over your shoulder.

"You should go first," you say, "since you're the one with the early warning system."

Go to 42.

"Watch my back," you say.
Go to 71.

46

The interior light in the refrigerator comes on when you open the door, and wow! That's a lot of white light. You can't see anything for a minute, and when your vision returns, you stare dumbly at the bright interior of the refrigerator. There's nothing here.

You close the refrigerator and stand quietly in the dark, letting your eyes adjust again. Your heart is pounding in your chest. Part of you had been anticipating something jumping out, either from the refrigerator itself or from somewhere else in the room. Hoping to catch you unaware.

But no. There's nothing. It's still a stripped-down kitchen with nothing but a new refrigerator in it.

Weird, huh?

You should leave it alone and move on. It's definitely a trap.
Go to 48.

What about the freezer drawer?
Go to 47.

47

You lean around the refrigerator and pull the power cord out of the wall. There's no reason for this thing to running. In fact, there shouldn't even be power coming into the house. Someone at the power company isn't paying attention. You don't care why this refrigerator is here, and you don't want to know what's in the freezer. The best way to deal with it is to do what you just did. Freezers only work when they have power.

It's too bad most situations aren't this easy to solve. Your job would be a lot easier.

You check out the narrow pantry. There's a wooden panel in the floor that leads down to a root cellar or something.

Go to 65.

You head efor the door that leads out to the hall. There's another room adjacent to the kitchen. Probably some kind of study.

Go to 67.

48

You close one eye as you pull out the freezer drawer. The glow isn't as bright as you expect it to be. Why? Because there's something in the freezer. It's black and gelatinous. Like moldy Jell-O or . . .

Oh shit, it's a shoggoth!

Even as you lurch back from the open freezer, the gelatinous mass uncurls. It flings tentacles out of the freezer. You knock one aside, but another one wraps around your other arm. It's got a tight grip, and as you struggle to pry it off, more tentacles wrap around you.

They're pulling you toward the freezer. You struggle to fight back, but it's really strong. You try to shove the drawer closed, but it pushes back with more tentacles.

You slam into the refrigerator, banging your head. A tentacle snakes up and around your neck. You can't breathe! More tentacles snake around your arms. It's pulling you down.

There's not enough space in that freezer compartment, but you realize the shoggoth doesn't care. You're going to fit, one way or another . . .

SPACE JELLIES ARE THE WORST.

ASSESSMENT SCORE: 25

Please refer to the Appendix for further information regarding your Assessment Score.

49

Pearson is banging on the walls of a tiny alcove under the stairs. There are a couple of wisps floating around his feet. "What?" He asks churlishly.

"Nothing," you say. "Just watching you work."

"The wall doesn't line up here," he says, indicating the alcove. It looks like it used to be a water closet. There are pipes coming out of the wall near the floor, and a metal cap has been put over the drain hole where the toilet used to be. "Got to be some sort of hidden passage or something."

"Sure," you say absently. You shine your light down the hallway, wondering what is at the back of the house. You see two more doors. You suspect one is the kitchen. "You check out the back of the house yet?"

He grunts, which isn't an answer. You swing your flashlight back to him.

"What?" he snaps.

You're about to say *Nothing* again, but realize doing so will turn this into a bad comedy sketch.

"You seeing things?" you ask instead.

He stops banging on the wall. "What kind of things?"

"Weird textures in the wallpaper. Ripples in the floor. Ecto-plasmic drips from the ceiling." You waggle your flashlight. "You know, the usual stuff."

"No," he says, and you don't like the way he's so quick to respond. "I'm not seeing any of that stuff."

There's something in the way he keeps moving his head back and forth that unsettles you. Or maybe you're still a little off from what you did or didn't see in the other room. "How about hearing things?" you ask.

"I'm fine," he snaps. "Stop with the fucking questions."

"Okay, okay," you say, putting up your hands.

He kicks one of the wisps and it bounces off the wall in the hall and rolls toward the kitchen.

"You gonna move or what?" He waves his hand at you—his right hand—and you stand your ground, giving him one of your infamous death stares. He has the presence of mind to look chagrined. "Sorry," he mutters. He tucks his gloved hand behind his back, putting it out of the way.

"Let's keep moving," you say, deciding it's not worth making a big deal out of things.
Go to 69.

"Let's just finish this," you say.
Go to 65.

50

Keeping your wits about you, you duck into the library on your left. There are built-in bookcases along the walls, and there is a stone hearth in the back of the room.

The best solution to the heebie-jeebies is to keep working, and you're not going to let some poltergeist action scare you off. Sure, you have no idea where your partner went, and—for now—you'll give him a pass on being an asshole and playing hide-and-go seek, but standing around and letting your knees knock together isn't getting the job done.

The shelves are empty. Not even a trashy gothic romance.

The hearth hasn't been used in some time either.

See? It's just an old house. No one cares. There's nothing to see here. Nothing weird went on. Pearson is just messing with you because he knows this is a shit assignment, and he's going to have a little fun. You can't say you haven't done the same.

Well, okay, you were young and dumb back then, and you do have some regrets about what happened, but it was a good lesson for everyone, wasn't it? It's not like anyone died or anything . . .

Investigate the hearth more closely.
Go to 75

Libraries that don't have any books are like trees without leaves. And now you're bummed out.
Go to 62.

51

You pick up your flashlight, and—let's be honest here—you're a little surprised when nothing untoward happens. The floor is a little uneven. That's all. There wasn't some psychokinetic forcefield that caused your flashlight to roll like that. It was just a warp in the floor. Nothing out of the ordinary for an old house.

In fact—watch this . . .

You go back to the bookcase and drop your flashlight again. It hits the floor, rotates about thirty degrees or so, and then stops.

It doesn't roll anywhere.

Son of a . . .

You're reaching into your jacket for your ceremonial knife when the floor collapses beneath you. You fall into a hole, but manage throw your arms out and catch yourself. You're dangling, and God knows what is down there beneath you. Your legs are kicking in empty space.

You dropped your knife when you fell. It's right over there. Not far from your flashlight. You might be able to reach it, but the floor is old and smooth beneath the dust. If you shift your grip, you might slip, and then were will you be?

No worse a situation than the one you're in already. You can hear the Old Man whispering in your head, like he's still alive. Still bitching at you for not learning the lesson. *You have no idea how deep this hole is. Or what lies at the bottom of it.*

You stop worrying about your knife.

There's nothing to grab on to. The only reason you haven't gone completely through the floor is because the hole is snug. If it were a little wider, you'd have fallen already. As it is, you aren't sure you can get a good enough purchase to pull yourself up and out of the hole.

Just breathe, you think. *Just take a second and focus.*

Something taps the bottom of your boot. Like a playful slap. You don't have a second . . .

Whatever it is touches you again, and it's not a slap this time. It's a grab.

Your coat tears as you are wrenched down. A shard of wood flooring slices your cheek.

Those are the last two things you remember. Thankfully . . .

YOU HAVE BEEN EATEN BY THE FLOOR. IT'S UNEXPECTED, BUT 'UNEXPECTED' COMES WITH THIS JOB.

ASSESSMENT SCORE: 43

Please refer to the Appendix for further information regarding your Assessment Score.

52

Keeping a tight grip on your flashlight, you turn counter clockwise three times, shaking off the phantasmal fingers of fear that are trying to get under your skin. Fear is part of the job. Fear isn't something that you let get the better of you. But that doesn't mean it won't try.

After the third rotation, you're feeling more centered. You don't sound like an elephant with a nasal infection when you exhale. The flashlight beam isn't jiggling when you shine it around the hall.

There. Better. You got this.

And when something laughs at you from upstairs, you don't immediately shit yourself.

You flick the light up. For a brief instant, you see a white face and then it is gone.

Was that Pearson? You can't be sure.

Charging up the stairs, you give chase.

At the top of the stairs, go left.
Go to 76.

No, wait. The other "left."
Go to 79.

53

"Really? The heart?" Archer chokes out a laugh. "You're going to remind *me* about going with your heart?"

You shake your head. "Now is not the time," you say.

"Oh? No? When is the time?"

You keep an eye on the phantom goats, which is mostly an excuse to not look at her. "Later," you say.

"Oh, of course. *Later.* I've heard that before."

"Look, right now we're working, and so maybe this isn't the best time to get all passive-aggressive with me."

"God, you are such a bitch," she mutters.

You see red for a second. The goats are all watching you. They seem very interested in whatever Archer has decided she needs to sort out *right the fuck now*. Seriously?

"I'm not the one who got all weak-kneed for Grankowski," you snap.

"No, you just seduced his wife," she retorts.

"After you fucked him!"

She looks at you, a wickedly perverse smile on her face. "And you know what? I liked it too," she says.

"God damnit, Archer." You try to control your temper. That was always an issue too, wasn't it? All those jealous rages. All those hours spent seething. Waiting. Wondering. *Knowing.*

It wasn't supposed to happen in the first place. The Night Office frowns on relationships between operatives. Emotional entanglement leads to vulnerability and inattentiveness. If you are too worried or wound up about the person you are working with, you won't be paying attention to things like—

Like the dark-eyed woman standing in the library. The one who all the goats are fawning around.

"Shit," you say, your anger draining away.

"Oh, dear," Archer says. She's seen the woman too. "Eliza . . ."

The creature inhabiting Eliza Zelphepjer makes the body smile. The goats start making eager noises. Hungry noises.

And then they attack . . .

EMOTIONAL BLACKMAIL AND REVENGE FUCKS ALWAYS COME BACK TO HAUNT YOU. PAYBACKS NEVER SOLVE ANYTHING.

ASSESSMENT SCORE: 41

Please refer to the Appendix for further information regarding your Assessment Score.

54

You find Archer in the room off the kitchen, a room which was probably a study once, but which has been turned into a solarium. Unlike everywhere else in the house, the windows haven't been boarded over. The outside of the solarium has been covered in a wire mesh, and there are heavy drapes on the inside that hide most of the broken windows.

Archer is standing next to a large mahogany desk in the corner of the room. There's a metal box on the desk, which she apparently found in one of the drawers. She's leafing though a journal which came out of the box.

"What did you find?"

"Eliza's journal," she says.

When you don't say anything, she looks up. "You didn't read the file, did you?"

"I looked at it," you say, trying not to be sound petulant.

"You didn't read it," she says. She shakes her head and returns her attention to the book. It's not personal, but at the same time, it's totally *personal*, isn't it?

You don't even want to deal with this right now. It's just like the last time you tried to bring this up with her. This . . . *non-work stuff.*

Ugh. You can't even say the words to yourself. For the eighteen millionth time, you castigate yourself for allowing anything to happen between the two of you. Operatives shouldn't get emotionally involved with other operatives. You'll make selfish choices, or you'll get caught up in worrying about what the other person in the relationship wants. Meanwhile, the rest of the world suffers because of your mental conflict. *You have to be ready to kill your own mother, if it means saving the universe,* the Old Man used to say. That's what working for the Night Office means. You have to be ready to do whatever it takes . . .

Of course, you didn't listen. You never do, and isn't that one of the things that drove her away?

When you turn around, Archer isn't there.

God, are you imaging all of this?
Go to 77.

No. You're not losing your mind. It's this house, and it's really starting to piss you off.
Go to 72.

55

"The black goat is the only one that is different," you say, waving a hand at the stuffed heads. "If they were hunting, why don't they have a Deep One? Or a shoggoth? Or—"

"Shoggoths turn to slush," Archer points out.

"Okay, not a shoggoth, but you know what I mean. Why don't they have other extra-dimensional critters?"

"Maybe they didn't get a chance to hunt anything else."

"Maybe they didn't," you say. "And if not, why not?"

Archer shrugs, and you stare at her. "Come on," you say. "You're the one who can find out the answers to these questions. You should go look."

She raises her shoulders. "I don't want to," she says. "There's something . . ."

"Not right about this place?" You shine the flashlight around the empty room. "I think you could say that about any job we take. They're all wrong. That's why we're here."

She shakes her head. "Don't be like that. That's not what I mean. There's something in the way."

You frown. "Lower-case 'way' or upper-case?" you ask. You couldn't quite tell from her tone.

"Lower-case," she says.

"That's odd. How does that work?"

"I don't know," she says. "That's why I'm concerned."

"Well, maybe we should take it as a sign to not ask too many questions," you say.

Go to 78.

"We should figure out what is blocking you and why," you say.
Go to 80.

56

Making things appear to disappear is the converse of creating mirages and illusion, and it is just as hard, if not harder. When someone suddenly disappears, it's not because they've scampered off without you noticing, it's because your perception of them has been compromised. Just as your brain gets confused and thinks you are seeing baby goats or six-eyed demons, your brain can lose track of what's right in front of you. Your eyes are passive receptors of light, which is to say that they see everything. What you *think* you *see* is a function of your brain making sense of all the sensory data.

It is said that native shamen were the only ones who could apprehend the European sailing ships when they landed in North and South America, because these mystics were the only ones who had trained their brains to not ignore visual objects that didn't have correlation in their mental stacks.

The influence in the house is trying to get tricky, but you're not an idiot. You've been around the block once or twice. You know how obscuration works.

You go to where Archer was standing earlier, half-expecting to bump into her, but you don't. You pause, fighting that niggling worm in the back of your head. The one saying, "This isn't an illusion!" You turn slowly, tracking the beam of your flashlight around the room.

There's no sign—

You stop.

The flashlight reflects back from the stainless steel surface of a tall refrigerator. It's very modern-looking, with the freezer on the bottom and a dispenser that puts out both ice and water. It gurgles as you look at it. Almost like it is laughing at you.

That was definitely not there a moment ago, your brain says, pointing out the obvious.

Against your better judgement and everything the Old Man taught you, you're going to open the refrigerator, aren't you?
Go to 81.

Oh, you're not falling for that one. You're going to steer clear of all illusionary appliances, thank you very much.
Go to 74.

57

"There was an . . . incident," Archer says. She's falling into the Way now, seeing back to when Zelphepjer Sr. was still alive. When hunting was on the agenda. "Both father and son were involved. There was"—Archer tilts her head—"a daughter. She was the one who practiced the arts. She knew how to open a portal, and her brother found out."

You nod, starting to see how the story went. "But instead of throwing her in the loony bin, they got her to let them through. So they could go hunting."

Archer nods. "Yes. She was their anchor. Until . . ." She covers her eyes and shakes her head.

You nod. You've heard versions of this story before. Someone discovers other realms exist. They make contact, and then get seduced by the limitless possibilities—money, sex, power. Though, in this case, it was the chance to hunt something no one else had ever seen. But they discover some of the creatures in this realm are hunters too. Creatures who find humanity fun and mutable, in the same way we used to have fun with Silly Putty when we were kids.

"She closed the portal," Archer says eventually. "While they were still on the other side."

"Good for her," you say.

Archer looks at you, anguish in her eyes. "Her father and brother," she says.

"Not anymore," you say. "She did the right thing."

"She couldn't handle it," Archer says. She approaches the altar and lays her hand on the torn cloth. "She killed herself here."

You don't have anything to say to that. All in all, it could have been a lot worse.

You hear boots on the gravel outside the shed, and you look over your shoulder to see Pearson. He's got cobwebs stuck in his hair, and the sleeve of his jacket is still smoking, but otherwise he looks unruffled. "I found a shoggoth," he says. He holds up his fingers, a centimeter or so apart. "Little one."

He peers into the shed and spots the array of stuffed heads. "That's creepy," he says.

"More tragic than creepy," you say.

Archer walks out of the shed without looking at either one of you.

"We done here?" Pearson asks.

"We're done," you say.

You haul the shed doors together and Close them tight. No one will know the truth of the Zelphepjer family tragedy, but that's the way it usually is when the Night Office is on the job.

A REAL TRAGEDY, BUT THAT'S YOUR STOCK AND TRADE, ISN'T IT? DON'T GET TOO WORKED UP OVER IT. THERE'LL BE ANOTHER ASSIGNMENT SOON ENOUGH.

ASSESSMENT SCORE: 73

Please refer to the Appendix for further information regarding your Assessment Score.

58

"Okay," you say as you start off into the maze. "Isn't there some rule about how to navigate through a maze?"

"You are thinking of labyrinths," Archer says. "Labyrinths have no dead ends, so to speak. Once you start walking one, you just have to keep turning the same way."

"Is that what Theseus did?"

You're referring to the old story about Theseus and the minotaur, though—now that you think about it—Theseus had help.

"Somewhat," she says. "Ariadne told him the secret of the labyrinth, but she gave him some thread as well. Just to be sure."

You eye the ground. "Too bad we can't leave marks."

"I'll remember it," she says. "It's easy for me to see the way we've come."

Head left.
Go to 83.

Head right.
Go to 89.

59

You indicate that Archer should go first, but she shakes her head. "I don't like being underground," she says.

You hesitate, trying to decide if this is something she is seeing or if this is an actual psychological reservation on her part. "What if I go?"

Worry lines etch themselves across her forehead, and there's a flutter in her hands. "If you—if you see a series of hexagonal stones, come back," she says.

"Okay," you say. "Anything else?"

"Fire," she whispers. "There will be fire."

"Great."

Thus warned, you descend into the hole. The ladder only has a dozen or so rungs before you feel solid ground beneath your feet. Keeping one hand on the ladder, you turn and examine the underground tunnel. It runs straight, more or less, and it feels like it is heading in the direction of the house.

You look up, and Archer is still there. "It goes that way," you say, pointing for her.

"Be careful," she says.

"I intend you," you say.

In fact . . .

You dig out the flare gun from one of your pockets and point it down the throat of the tunnel. You pull the trigger, and the ruddy flare sputters down the tunnel, leaving a trail of sparks in its wake. It hits a wall and bounces. You lose track of it, but it hasn't gone far. Its flickering glow lights up a large room.

You reload the flare gun as you head toward the room. There's a slight incline, and the walls are supported with wooden slats and concrete blocks. It's a little dry, and you spot mushrooms growing in several spots, but overall, whoever dug this tunnel knew what they were doing.

There are a pair of steps leading down to the room at the end of the tunnel. The ceiling is a meter or so higher than the tunnel. The floor has been covered with granite slabs, and smaller slabs have been placed along the wall. There's an altar on your right, and on your left, there's a pedestal of some kind.

Inspect the altar first.
Go to 85.

Start with the slab.
Go to 87.

60

You and Archer head down the path between the hedges. The ground is covered with packed dirt, and if there were indicators on the hedges that helped guide you through the maze, they are gone now. When the path turns suddenly, you lose track of the moon.

After a few more steps, the hedge maze opens up to a small clearing, where there's a stone bench. You could sit, but you want to keep moving. You have a bad feeling about this maze.

"Which way?" you ask Archer.

"Left," she says. "You should always go left."
Go to 86.

"Right," she says. "It's important to alternate which direction you go."
Go to 88.

"I'm not sure," she says. "This doesn't seem right."
Go to 58.

61

You crab-walk toward the spot where you saw the glitter, shining your light ahead of you. You get to the corner and find nothing but some narrow cracks in the wall.

Rats, you think. *That's all it was.*

Shaking your head at how jumpy you've gotten, you swivel around, orienting yourself back toward the entrance of the root cellar.

Your flashlight beam picks up more glittering points. Lots more . . .

Rats, your brain registers. *It's definitely rats.*

Holding your light in one hand, you fumble in your jacket with the other, looking for that damn charm that repels rodents. Which pocket did you put it in? Now is not the time to get confused about your organizational schemas.

The rats make a noise like a flock of birds swarming into a stark winter sky. There's one climbing your leg! Where did he come from?

You shake him off, but he's replaced by two more. One of them bites you on the calf. By St. Malone's third nipple, that hurts!

You bring your hand out of your jacket and you thrust the object at the rats. It doesn't have any effect, and with growing horror, you realize you've pulled the ginger charm—a piece of ginger that has been charged in the likeness of a man. It's old-school homeopathic magic, the sort Frazer used to go on and on about. But it works against serpents, not rats.

One of the little monsters climbs onto your outstretched hand and bites your knuckles. You smash your hand against the ground, and something snaps inside the rat. It shrieks in pain. You get a momentary surge of adrenaline from the sound.

Except that sound is also a rallying cry for the rest of them.

You can't fight them all. You struggle toward the hatch that leads back to the pantry. Surely you can get out of the root cellar?

There are more of them swarming out of the walls. You can't put your feet or hands anywhere without hitting a squirming body. They're going to overwhelm you in a second . . .

THERE ARE RATS IN THE WALLS—A GIVEN IN THIS BUSINESS. RATS ARE EASY TO CO-OPT AND TURN INTO MURDEROUS HORDES.

ASSESSMENT SCORE: 32

Please refer to the Appendix for further information regarding your Assessment Score.

62

You return to the foyer. It still looks like someone has come through here, but whether that's Pearson or you is hard to distinguish at this point. The wallpaper is still drab. The front door is still closed. Not many choices here, are there?

Check out the hall.
Go to 41.

Venture to the right where the sitting room and dining room are located.
Go to 25.

Quit dawdling and head upstairs.
Go to 90.

You've had enough of this job.
Go to 64.

63

When you put the book back on the shelf, you accidentally drop your flashlight. It rolls across the floor along a weird path, like there is something warped under the floor. Your flashlight comes to a stop near the center of the room.

You make no move toward it. In fact, you're holding your breath. The last time something like this happened, you nearly got flayed alive by a tentacled monstrosity from an alternate dimension. Something with more teeth than brains. It was like those fish that swim at twenty thousand feet below the ocean's surface. The ones with little light lures they use to hypnotize stupid fish.

You stand still and wait. Eventually, you release the breath you've been holding, but you are very quiet as you do it. Nothing moves, but you stay still awhile longer anyway. Just in case . . .

Is it safe?
Go to 51.

Your flashlight is pointing toward the hearth. Curious.
Go to 92.

64

You tear your jacket as you squeeze out the window in the front room. A pocket is ripped, and whatever you had in there is gone. You do a quick inventory of your other pockets. Oh, it's just a vial of blessed salt. Eyeing the jagged hole of the window, you decide it's not worth going back in for. You have a large jar of it at home, anyway.

Speaking of home, this job has been a joke from the start. Both your partners wandered off, and there was no sign of anything going on inside that warrants you being here. In less that twenty-four hours, the place is going to be torn down anyway. Three months from now, there's going to be a shopping mall here. Even if there are lingering haunts, they're going to be buried beneath several tons of concrete. Almost as good a solution as having a Closer purge the place.

You straighten your jacket and head for your car. For some reason, your thoughts to turn to frozen yogurt. As you drive away from the Zelphepjer House, you're think about stopping at the store and getting a pint or two. Would Mr. Fish like pistachio lemon or blue raspberry?

Aw, heck. Why not get both?

THIS IS THE 'I'D RATHER HAVE ICE CREAM' ENDING.

ASSESSMENT SCORE: N/A
PLEASE SEE THE PROCTOR.

Please refer to the Appendix for further information regarding your Assessment Score.

65

There's a short ladder going down into the root cellar, which is only a few feet below the ground floor. You duck down and shine your light around.

The cellar isn't very big, and from the looks of it, it hasn't been used for a long time. Modern refrigeration got us out of the basement, after all, and you doubt they were storing much in this dark hole.

You sweep your light back and forth one last time, making sure there's nothing of interest. You catch a glint of light off to the left, and the hair on the back of your neck tickles. Something is watching you.

Naturally, you're going to have to take a closer look, right?
Go to 61.

Yeah, no. It's just a couple of rats.
Go to 82.

66

You look at Archer. "Secret basement under the utility shed," you say. "You got any insight?"

She shivers slightly and gets that faraway look in her eye. "It was used for storage," she says. "During Prohibition. They were . . . bootleggers. I see casks being lowered. Forgotten. No one opened the door for a long time. I see men with tools, digging deeper. Farther. Yes. They're expanding the room now. They are bringing more supplies. I see copper rods. Half moons that glitter. They're . . . more circles. Down in the secret room."

This is more like it. Secret rooms. Ritual chambers.

"All right," you say. "I think we found what we are looking for." You fish a few glow sticks out of your jacket and shake them to life. You drop them into the hole, and they lie at the bottom of the shaft, like a dismal casting of runes.

You climb down. The tunnel is tall enough that you can stand. When you orient yourself, you realize the passage runs away from the house.

You duck and walk along the tunnel. Your light reveals a large room. The walls and floor are covered with wood paneling. Faded rugs are scattered on the floor, and your flashlight beam picks up the dull shine of copper along the edges of some of the rugs. You shove one of the rugs back, and reveal the curved edge of a magic circle, inlaid into the wood.

There are two alcoves in the room, which is longer than it is wide. Each alcove contains a statue on a pedestal, and when you look more closely, you realize the figures aren't human.

Of course they aren't, you think.

The one on the left is the Keeper, an entity in vogue about sixty years ago. Back when the world was in the grip of the Cold War, and worrying about nuclear annihilation was the national pastime. Lots of people built bunkers and fallout shelters and places like this: subterranean shrines where they worshiped gods that might save them from atomic fire.

Though, the Keeper never kept anyway safe, did he?

The one on the right is from a pantheon of cosmic horrors that exist so far outside of time and space that they might as well be unintelligible. Worshipping a god like this was like a flea worshipping an aircraft carrier. One could barely conceptualize the other, and the other would never—*ever*—notice a fawning supplicant.

Archer comes into the chamber. She glances at the Keeper, but doesn't give it any more attention than that. She comes over to where you are standing and looks at the statue in the alcove behind you. "Oh, that's—" And she says the name of the Elder God.

"Don't do that," you hiss.

"What? Say its name?" She shrugs. "It can't hear us."

"I know. It's just—" You try to shake off your annoyance.

She extends her arms and slowly turns in a circle. "This is where they did it," she says. "There are ripples here. They're all coming from this room."

"Okay then," you say. "This is where I'll do my part too."

You get out what you're going to need from your pockets. Chisel. Hammer. Vial of mercury. Salt tablets. Consecrated hosts. Spray paint. "I'll get started."

You're thorough, and it takes about an hour to desecrate the statues, crack the circles on the floor, and salt the atmosphere in the room. When you are done, you head back to the ladder where Archer is waiting for you.

"All set?" she asks.

You get the pair of phosphorus grenades out of your jacket. "Just about," you say.

Archer doesn't need any more prompting than that. She scampers up the ladder.

You pull the pins on the grenades and roll them toward the ritual chamber. You go up the ladder as the grenades go off. There's a whoof of noise from the tunnel.

Before too much smoke gets out, you and Archer drops the hatch. After that, you Close the hatch for good, making sure no one can undo the destruction you've done.

"That's that," you say when you finish. "Call it in."

Archer flashes you a smile, which makes it all worthwhile.

A CLOSER HAS NO COMPUNCTION ABOUT BURNING IT ALL DOWN, SALTING THE EARTH, AND COVERING UP THEIR HANDIWORK. NO ONE EVER NEED KNOW.

ASSESSMENT SCORE: 84

Please refer to the Appendix for further information regarding your Assessment Score.

67

Tucked behind the staircase is a short corridor that leads you to a narrow room that has been modified into a glass-enclosed solarium. The windows take up the far wall and a portion of the sloping ceiling, though everything has been covered with heavy drapes and plywood boards.

At the near end of the room is a heavy desk—large enough that you wonder how they got it through the door in the first place. There is a distressed bundle underneath it, like a family of foxes had made a nest once upon a time. Mama fox fed her babies until they were big enough to fend for themselves.

You inspect the desk, and find all of the drawers empty. Well, except for the bottom drawer on the left. It's locked. Or maybe it is jammed. It's hard to tell.

Where's an Opener when you need one?

Pearson's disappearance is getting bothersome.

Force open the drawer.
Go to 84.

There's no point in breaking up the desk because whatever is in that drawer has probably turned into poisonous mold anyway.
Go to 91.

68

Upstairs is all bedrooms—master on the left, three smaller rooms on the right. You walk through them and find them empty. "What a fucking waste of time," Pearson says when you rejoin him on the upstairs landing.

You nod in agreement.

"Hey, you guys find anything?" Archer is down in the foyer. "There's a hedge maze out back. It's pretty cool."

"Did you—" You stop when Pearson looks at you. You shake your head and focus on the job. "We're clear," you say.

You hear Archer echo your pronouncement, and Pearson's face relaxes. "Clear," he says, completing the ritual. The site has been Opened. The Way has been cleared. The Closer has spoken.

"Have fun writing up the report," Pearson says as he brushes past you.

That is the one thing that sucks about being the Closer: the paperwork. Since you're the one who ultimately decides if a site has been cleared or not, it's your signature on the paperwork. While the other two are done for the night, you've got another hour or two to go. All those damn forms.

NO ONE WANTS TO BE A CLOSER. BUT SOMEONE HAS TO DO THE PAPERWORK.

ASSESSMENT SCORE: N/A
PLEASE SEE THE PROCTOR.

Please refer to the Appendix for further information regarding your Assessment Score.

69

The room behind the kitchen is a small study that has been turned into a solarium. All the windows have been covered with plywood. In the corner opposite the door is a big mahogany desk—much too big to fit through the door. It looks like a family of foxes made a nest under it a while ago, but there's no sign any of them have been back in a year or more.

You check the drawers. They're all empty, except the lower lefthand one. It's locked.

Where's an Opener when you need one?

Wait for Pearson.
Go to 93.

Waiting is what you do for laundry. Pry the drawer open.
Go to 96.

70

You go over to the refrigerator and the open freezer drawer. There's nothing in the drawer, obviously, because it's occupant has already jumped out and is busy trying to savage your partner.

You glance over your shoulder to see how he is doing with the shoggoth, and you're surprised to see Pearson lying on his side. There's no sign of the shoggoth, which is a bad sign, actually. There should be some crispy bits from Pearson zapping it with his Hand.

You slam the freezer drawer shut. Reaching into your jacket for your ceremonial knife, you approach Pearson's body with some caution. There's one place where the shoggoth could have gone, and if it did, then that's not Pearson on the floor.

Sure enough, he sits up suddenly. His eyes are splotchy with burst blood vessels, and when he hisses at you, his tongue is black. "Son of a bitch," you curse. What kind of first-year idiot lets a shoggoth eat his brain?

Pearson reaches for you with his Hand. It sparks and buzzes with power. Oh, he's not touching you with that. You stab him in the palm with the iron blade. You feel a tingle going up your arm, but it's not anywhere near a full pulse of Opener magic.

Pearson's other hand snakes out and grabs your ankle. Damnit! You weren't expecting that. Before you can pull away, he yanks and you go down hard. He's on you in a flash, moving with spider-like agility. His normal hand is strong, but it's the other one you are worried about. The one with the knife sticking out of it. He's oblivious to the blade, however, and when he tries to grab your shoulder, the blade is pressed deeper into his Hand. Like a plunger. It would be funny—sort of—if the brush of his gloved fingers weren't making your jacket smoke.

This isn't good. Even with your iron knife in his hand, he's still putting power through the Hand. You struggle to get away from him, but he's a heavy weight on your legs and hips.

You get both hands on his wrist. With a sudden shove, you push his arm back. He realizes what you are doing and jerks away. The blade misses his face, but you drive it into the fleshy part of his throat. He shrieks—a sound like dying animals and fingernails on chalkboards. Damnit, you missed his esophagus.

He's still on you, though, and now he's thrashing about like a crazed sea lion. You can't get a grip on the knife hilt sticking out of his palm.

He claws at you with his left hand, his fingers digging into your neck. His eyes are wide and his mouth is gaping open. There's something moving in the back of his throat. His shoulders tense, and before you can get him off you, he heaves up the contents of his stomach.

But it's not partially digested food. It's something dark and sticky and filled with too many eyes. It splashes all over your face. You press your lips together tightly and squeeze your eyes shut. But it's no good. It can still get in through your nose and your ears.

Its touch is cold . . .

NEVER TURN YOUR BACK ON A SHOGGOTH. THIS WAS COVERED IN YOUR ORIENTATION LITERATURE.

ASSESSMENT SCORE: 27

Please refer to the Appendix for further information regarding your Assessment Score.

71

You and Pearson head for the kitchen. You go in first, which is dumb since you're the Closer, but you try not to overthink your plan of action here. Mostly, you're just pissed at Pearson and want some distance from him before you say or do something stupid.

Anyway, there's not much to the kitchen. It's been stripped bare, down to the countertops and outlets. You figure tweakers have yanked all the wire out of the walls. Even if there was power to the building, there's nothing in the walls that'll get juice to an appliance.

The back wall had picture windows and a nice set of French doors, once upon a time. Now it's a rough facade of plywood and 2 x 4s. The pleasant decor of the soon-to-be-demolished house.

Nothing stirs. Not even a dust bunny.

Over in the corner is a small pantry. In the floor is a wooden trapdoor, which seems out of place in a home like this, but—given its size and location—probably leads to a root cellar.

"This place is deserted," Pearson mutters. You're inclined to agree with him, but aren't about give him the satisfaction of being right.

You flick your light over the trapdoor in the pantry. "Root cellar," you note. "You want to check it out?"

"No," Pearson says.

Well, if the Opener isn't going to open the hatch, why should you? You're the Closer. Might as well do you job.

The trapdoor has a padlock clasp. You flick it. Cheap, but serviceable. You've worked with worse. It'll do.

You get out your kit from the hidden pockets in your jacket, and while Pearson wanders around, thumping on the walls like a fucking idiot, you melt the clasp into something resembling a blob of sealing wax. Using your Seal, you lock that trapdoor forever. The metal hisses and bubbles, but when it stops being fussy, the impression is good and clear.

"Done," you say.

Check the room next to the kitchen.
Go to 69.

It's definitely time to check upstairs.
Go to 68.

72

What if I'm imaging all of this?

The thought keeps following you around the house. In every room, you find something that reminds you of Archer. More than once, you catch yourself talking to her as if she is there. Sometimes she is, but everytime you turn your back, she vanishes again.

It dawns on you slowly, mostly because you don't want to face the truth. You're not on assignment. You're not wandering around this old house. It's all in your head.

You have to be imagining all of this.

You end up back in the study.

The box is still on the desk. When you open it, the journal is there. You recognize it, even though you haven't seen it in many years. You pick it up and page through it. You know whose handwriting that is, don't you? You read some of the entries, and they're like dreams you can't remember having. You don't remember writing anything down—not like this. You know better than to write things like this down.

I didn't do any of this! you think.

Near the back of the book, you find the entry where you first met Archer. That's the straw that breaks you. You crumble to the floor, clutching the journal to your chest, sobbing like a child.

You remember why you stopped writing in this journal. First you met her, and then—*oh, it's only a few pages more, isn't it?* And then she was gone.

All that remains of her is what you wrote in this journal.

"No," you scream. "This isn't right. This isn't the truth."

She's still alive. She has to be.

Otherwise . . .

She's dead, Eliza, the Old Man says. *You have to let her go. You have to come back to us.*

You shake your head. "No," you snarl. "I'm not going to forget her. I'm not going to let go."

You have to, the Old Man says, but you don't want to listen to him any more. You push him out of your head. You push him out of everything . . .

It's just you and her.

You hold the journal tight. Just you and her.

Okay, the Old Man says, *let's reset it.*

His voice is louder. It's all around you. You sit up, looking around you wildly. Wondering how you can still be hearing him. You pushed him out. This is your place. He can't be—

Let's try this again, he says.

OCCUPATIONAL MENTAL THERAPY AND PSYCHOLOGI-CAL RE-ALIGNMENT TREATMENTS—INCLUDING NEXT-GEN IMMERSIVE VIRTUAL REALITY SIMULATION SESSIONS—ARE AVAILABLE TO ALL FIELD AGENTS AND ARE PART OF THE CORE BENEFITS PACKAGE OFFERED BY NIGHT OFFICE ASSET RESOURCE MANAGEMENT.

ASSESSMENT SCORE: N/A
PLEASE SEE THE PROCTOR.

Please refer to the Appendix for further information regarding your Assessment Score.

73

Closers, on the other hand, approach things with a little more finesse. Well, more *burn it all down and salt the earth* style of finesse.

You retrieve a bottle of thrice-blessed salt from your coat—that stuff you get from the mail-order company out of York Factory in Manitoba. You unseal the bottle and sprinkle some over the writhing mass of Pearson and the shoggoth. The space jelly reacts immediately to the purified salt. You can almost hear its psychic scream as its cells are dehydrated into nothingness.

Not really, of course. Shoggoths don't have vocal cords. Or pain receptors. But still, the implosive contact between salt and shoggoth is so intensive that it is almost physical.

It tries to wrap itself around Pearson's head, as if you won't keep sprinkling it out of concern for injuring your partner.

Oh, it's so cute, isn't it? Like worrying about burning Pearson is going to slow you down . . .

Keep sprinkling.
Go to 97.

You might actually have an empathic bone in your body. Somewhere. Hold that thought . . .
Go to 94.

74

You steer clear of the refrigerator as you try to trace back everything that has happened since you entered the house. Clearly, the influence within these walls is affecting your ability to reason and think clearly. First, there were the goats in the front room. Then you lost Archer, but gained a refrigerator.

You go back to the foyer, where the front door is stuck shut.

Of course it is, you think. This place isn't done with you yet.

You check the other rooms of the ground floor. The library is still dusty and empty, and the sitting room's wallpaper is still drab and peeling. No sign of your teammates.

You know you're being watched. You can feel it like a warm breath of air. You lift your flashlight and shine it upstairs.

A pale face with dead eyes and a bloody mouth is caught for a second in your flashlight's beam, and it is gone. You hear the sound of someone running upstairs.

You jerk the flashlight toward the sitting room, and there's another floating mask there. This one's mouth is frozen in a horrible scream. It darts toward the dining room before you can do anything.

When you shine the light down the hall toward the kitchen, you spot another face down by the floor. It scuttles away like a spider.

Something laughs softly in the library.

It wants you to spook, but why not show it you know what you are doing? It's in the library. Deal with it.

Go to 99.

Enough of this chasing your own tail bullshit.

Go to 144.

75

The mantel over the hearth is made from a solid piece of walnut. When you shine your light on it, there's a spot that glints. It's more polished than the surrounding wood, as if it has been rubbed quite frequently. You test the spot with your thumb and there's a little give in the wood. When you press harder, something clicks behind the wall.

The bookcase next to the hearth pops away from the wall. Ooh, a secret passage!

You step off the hearth and pull the hidden door open. Your flashlight reveals a narrow passage, and at the end of the passage, there are steps going down.

This is more like it!

You duck into the passage and head downstairs.

Go to 115.

76

You dash up the stairs after the mysterious apparition. You think it went left, and so you hustle across the second floor landing in that direction. A set of double doors lead to a spacious master bedroom. There's a walk-in closet and a separate bathroom. Crusted water marks stain the ceiling. All the angles are tidy and square, making it difficult to hide from the beam of your flashlight.

There's an old cast-iron tub in the bathroom—one with taloned feet. You can imagine that bathtub animating—in fact, didn't that happen to a team up in Dorchester? You opt to leave the bathroom alone for the moment.

In the back of the walk-in closet, you find a cedar chest. It looks new, of course, but you're not fooled. They want to blend in, but not so well that you don't notice them.

The chest is big enough to hold a body.

You keep your distance.

"Not a very good hiding place," you say.

Something creaks in the bathroom.

Start with the creepy noise. Investigate the bathroom.
Go to 95.

The creepy noise is meant to distract you. Don't fall for it.
Go to 87.

77

Standing there, in the cold study, you realize Archer couldn't be on this job. She's been dead for over a year now. Because of what happened in East Montook. Because of what you failed to do.

There wasn't a third operative on this mission. It was just you and Pearson, which is why he got pissed when you went on and on about Archer. That's why he went on ahead, because he knew you were just losing your shit.

They all know, don't they? Management doesn't want you in the field anymore. But until a spot opens up in Accounting, what are they going to do? This is why they only allow you for milk runs like this, and even easy jobs like this are too much for you to handle.

Makes you wonder what Pearson did to fuck up so badly that he got babysitting duty, doesn't it?

You wander out of the study. The house is empty. It's all cold and dark. There's nothing here. It's just an old mansion scheduled to be torn down. There was never any evil influence or animal sacrifices being carried out in the pool. It's just a sad old house, waiting to be torn down. Waiting to be thrown out.

Just like you.

You go and sit down on the porch step. The moon is still high in sky, and you watch the shadows play in the yard. After awhile, Pearson comes out and sits beside you on the step.

He rolls one of his noxious cigarettes and lights it. You cough, even though none of the smoke is drifting in your direction.

"You okay?" he asks.

"No," you say, fighting the urge to hug yourself.

"I'll say you did good on my report," he says.

You nod, tucking your chin against your knees. "She was back there," you say. "In the pool."

He doesn't say anything. You figure he's read the report. *Of course she was in the pool*, you think. *That's where they found her body.*

"You should go home," Pearson says.

"Home," you whisper. Mr. Fish will be waiting for you.

You start to cry. You can't help it.

You tried to save part of her, but it didn't work. Mr. Fish isn't the same, even if he does smell like her. That has to be enough. Otherwise, what else is there to live for?

THE NIGHT OFFICE PREFERS ITS OPERATIVES AVAIL THESMELVES OF IN-HOUSE OCCUPATIONAL THERAPY AND PSYCHOLOGICAL RE-ALIGNMENT SOLUTIONS IN ORDER TO MAINTAIN THEIR SANITY. HOWEVER, IF A HOMEOPATHIC HOME REMEMDY WORKS, THE NIGHT OFFICE WILL TURN A BLIND EYE . . .

ASSESSMENT SCORE: N/A
PLEASE SEE THE PROCTOR.

Please refer to the Appendix for further information regarding your Assessment Score.

78

Archer likes your idea, and she leaves the shed. You play your light across the dead animals for a moment. Before your imagination gets too wound up, you leave the shed too.

While you are laying out your tools, Archer hauls the heavy door shut. You set the seal with sulphur and write a long explanation in cryptic glyphs with your Sharpie along the edge of the two doors. Using your mercury dropper, you fuse the ends of the chain together, and then you finish the job with a proper Closing incantation.

When you are done, you join Archer who has wandered back to the pool. "It's Closed," you tell her.

She is looking at the copper circle in the pool. "It's not over," she says. "Whatever they summoned is still out there. It wasn't just the goat. It was something else."

You look toward the house where Pearson is still, presumably, wandering around, looking for weird mushrooms and stains that shouldn't exist in this reality. "Is it in the house?"

She shakes her head. "It's long gone."

"But not from this world."

"No," she says. "It's still here."

You lift your gaze to the moon. "I'm sure it'll turn up eventually," you say. "Evil always does."

THE NIGHT OFFICE DOES NOT GIVE UP. EVER.

ASSESSMENT SCORE: 72

Please refer to the Appendix for further information regarding your Assessment Score.

79

You run up the stairs. At the top, there is a wide landing with a pair of plywood-covered French doors that probably take you to an open deck. Double doors lead to your left, and on the right, there is a short hallway. You quickly assess that neither the plywood-covered doors nor the doors to your left have been disturbed. That leaves the hallway.

The hall runs a couple of meters and then cuts right. There's a room on the left that doesn't have a door. Judging from the layout of the house, there are two—maybe, three—more rooms past the turn in the hall. Smaller bedrooms, you suspect. There will be closets, of course. All sorts of spots for someone to jump out at you.

Room sweeping is such a pain in the ass.

You check the room on the left, sweeping your light around the empty space. Nothing in the room itself. The closet is missing one of its accordian doors, which makes it easy to check.

Peering around the corner of the hall, you spot three more rooms. They all have doors.

There's no sign of Pearson, or anyone else.

Go to the door on the left.
Go to 100.

Try the door at the end of the hall.
Go to 101.

How about the door on the right?
Go to 161.

80

"I'm right here," you say to Archer. You touch her arm and offer her a smile when she looks at you. She tries to smile back, but she isn't as sure as you are. You squeeze her arm. "I'm not going anywhere," you say, and you realize you mean it.

You and Archer found each other at a time when you were both vulnerable. You were coming off that relationship with Cee Cee, and she had just realized how empty and loveless her marriage to Roderick was. The first time was an accident—one that you both swore would not happen again—but after the second time, she was the one who gave voice to the attraction that was undeniable between both of you. Even though relationships between operatives was frowned upon, you two managed to find a way to be together. For awhile, it was really nice.

Until it wasn't. You knew the risks. The psychological scars of what you do for a living make it hard to sustain human bonds. You both tried really hard. For awhile, you thought you were going to beat the odds. But you didn't. After a shouting match when you both said things that couldn't be taken back, she left.

You have little recollection of the next six months—on and off the job. It wasn't until you fucked up Closing that barn in Connecticut that you started to pay attention again. The Old Man said you had two choices. *It'll be tracking staple use for Standards and Practices,* he had said. *Or*—he had paused for dramatic effect—*you'll be dead.*

I'm dead either way, so what's the difference? you had snapped at him. You were still too raw to deal with it.

Get a plant, he said. *Get two. I don't care. Find something you can take care of.*

That was how you found Mr. Fish.

While he was good for you, he didn't replace human contact. Over the last few months, you've realized how much you miss the touch of another human being. Maybe a new relationship wouldn't end up like you and Archer. Or . . . and you can't believe you're considering this . . .

Or, maybe the two of you could try again.

In that moment—when you re-examine your choices during the last year—you realize Archer is doing the same thing.

"Okay," she says. She reaches over and puts her hand over yours. "I know."

Of course she knows. That thought makes you want to laugh, but before you can, the world turns inside out. Everything gets white along the edges, and the stuffed animal heads on the wall smear like melting clocks. Except for their eyes. Their eyes remain fixed. Wide and staring.

Next to you, Archer is glowing. Her hair is like white fire.

The altar has gone black, and thin tendrils drift up from it in defiance of gravity.

Archer lifts her arm and points. Your head is very heavy, but you manage to look. She's pointing along a fourth-dimensional axis. You peer into the infinite vale of time. It's dizzying how it telescopes away from you as you try to focus on it.

She grabs her hand. *Not that far*, she says.

The black goat head starts to bray with laughter. When you look back, the whole wall is gone. The rest of the heads are streamers of light and darkness. Their eyes still stare at you, though. Hard points, among the smeared reality.

The black goat hasn't changed. In fact, there's a shadow growing out of the stump. A shadow that looks more upright and bipedal than four-legged.

Hang on. This is going to get wild.
Go to 102.

You've seen enough. Pull Archer back.
Go to 103.

81

It is difficult to sustain a sense of disbelief when you are deep in the mind-bending horror fest that is a Night Office job. You have to remember the reality we choose to believe is consensual, and that it is based on a very narrow understanding of the universe. When you see things that shouldn't exist, the screws anchoring your sense of self start to unwind. After awhile, one of them comes out; soon, another follows, and then all that's keeping you anchored is the reminders you surround yourself with. The things that tell you that *yes, this is all true*, and *no, that is total lunacy.*

Which is why you keep Mr. Fish around, isn't it? He helps remind you that the world is totally broken. That everything you know and believe is a lie. That nothing is true, and everything is possible.

And this refrigerator—this gleaming modern appliance—shouldn't be in this house. It shouldn't be drawing power because you know damn well all the wiring was stripped out months ago by junkies looking for a way to score a fix. This refrigerator is part of the lie.

And yet, you're going open it anyway, aren't you?

You're going to find something horrible inside. You know you will. There will be something nestled there that will help you re-anchor yourself. There must be. Ever since she looked into the future, everything has been—*no, it was the past! No, don't let this happen*—ever since she stepped on the Way, everything has been . . .

Just open the refrigerator. Everything will make sense again.
This isn't real. This is not happening!
She made this happen. It's her fault.
Reality gets thin, doesn't it?
Just open the refrigerator.

You know what you're going to find, don't you?

Mr. Fish has been hungry lately, and he's very particular about what he eats. These jobs are always a good way for you to bring home some fresh meat for him.

Open the door.

You know what you need . . .

In the back of your mind, you hear baby goats laughing.

CREEPY GOATS MAKE EVERYTHING CREEPIER. IT GETS TO WHERE YOU CAN'T EVEN TRUST YOURSELF, DOESN'T IT?

ASSESSMENT SCORE: 38

Please refer to the Appendix for further information regarding your Assessment Score.

82

You climb out of the root cellar. After closing the wooden door, you weave a tiny spell to make sure it stays Closed. Just in case.

You return to the foyer. It's still empty and dusty, which is a relief, in a way. You wouldn't want to come back here and find fresh tracks. Like something is cleverly stalking you. That hasn't happened in a while . . .

Anyway, what's left?

Check out the room in the back of the hall.
Go to 67.

Check out the library.
Go to 39.

The ground floor is clear. Time to check upstairs.
Go to 90.

Actually, the whole house is clear. You can say that with a degree of confidence. Not one hundred percent, but enough to sign off on your report.
Go to 64.

83

There's a mummified bird hanging from a branch that sticks out like an accusatory finger in the next clearing.

"I feel like we've been here already," you say.

Archer cocks her head to the side, listening intently. "We may have been," she says. "There are many overlaps here."

"Wonderful," you say.

Keep going left.
Go to 104.

Switch it up and go right.
Go to 106.

84

You take out the drawer above the lower drawer and shine your light into the desk. Sure enough, there's no panel between drawers, and you can see down in the locked drawer.

There's a metal box inside the drawer. You tuck your flashlight under your chin and use both hands to get the box out of the lower drawer. It takes a bit of maneuvering, but you manage. You put the box on the desk and inspect it.

It's a dull metal lockbox. You could probably pop the lock with your thumb. In fact, you do so. Inside you find a leather-bound book, wrapped with a heavy strand of rawhide.

It's in good shape, all things considered, and it contains a number of dated entries, scrawled in black ink by a precise hand.

Skim over the journal.
Go to 105.

Take the journal with you. You can read it later.
Go to 107.

85

You examine the slab and discover it's not a solid piece of marble. It's a casket. There are indentations on the top. Four of them, all in a line. When you inspect them more closely, you find they are deeper than you thought. In fact, they probably go all the way though the lid. They're not natural. They've been purposely drilled. *Almost like . . .*

You try to stop this thought from forming, but it gets past your defenses.

. . . air holes.

They're hexagonal in shape.

You stumble away from the casket, nearly tripping over the flare as you do.

It's a sarcophagus. You realize the holes aren't just for air. *You could pour blood into them too.*

You stare at the sarcophagus, and you wonder how thick its walls are. How tight is that lid . . . ?

Something moves in the room with you. You whirl around, but there's no one there. You didn't actually hear anything, but nonetheless, something moved.

Time to go, you think. You walk quickly back to the ladder and clamber up. Archer jerks in surprise when you spring out of the hole. You motion for her to help you with the trapdoor, and the two of you slam the hatch shut.

You write twice as many Wards as necessary with your Sharpie, and you scatter all the salt and sulphur you have with you. Three drops of blood from your finger, and the magic starts to coalesce. You pop the Closing Seal into existence with a fierce thought, and only then do you finally relax.

"That bad?" Archer asks quietly.

You nod, hoping that the sarcophagus was empty. If it wasn't, you Closed the tunnel as best you could. When they build a shopping mall on the piece of land, you hope they pour a lot of concrete in this area. Keep whatever is down there sealed away for a long, long time.

A CLOSER'S JOB IS TO MAKE SURE NOTHING GETS THROUGH. THAT'S ALL THAT MATTERS. IF YOU LEAVE SOMETHING ALIVE AND ENTOMBED FOREVER, THAT COUNTS AS A WIN.

ASSESSMENT SCORE: 79

Please refer to the Appendix for further information regarding your Assessment Score.

86

You navigate around a corner and down a narrow path between hedges. It's starting to all look the same. "We've been here before," you say to Archer.

"Nonsense," she says.

You're not so sure, and by the time you reach the next inter-section, you're pretty sure you've been here already.

Head left.
Go to 108.

Head right.
Go to 109.

87

The problem with hiding in a confined space in a room that has no other viable hiding places is that everyone knows where you are hiding. What is Pearson thinking? The chest has a lid, which means it can be Closed.

Pearson knows what you can do, so he's either not himself—i.e., compromised by an alien intelligence—or he knows he's compromised, and he's trying to make it easy for you.

Everyone loses their mind eventually. It's part of the job. No one retires. You get retired by another operative when your mind snaps. The best you can hope for is the team does their job quickly and efficiently. No one likes a lot of pain.

You take out the canister of wax seals from your jacket. You get two seals out of the canister and slap them on the chest. Using your ceremonial knife, you ignite one with drops of your blood. The chest flexes as the seal clamps down. From inside, you hear a muffled shout.

"Sorry, Pearson," you say. He's a big man, and the chest is less than a meter square. There's no way he could fit in there, even if he was a professional contortionist. He had help, which is to say that something foul took over his brain and shut down all his pain receptors. He didn't notice when an eldritch intelligence broke his bones in order to fit inside that cramped space.

A few more drops of blood activates the other seal. The chest vibrates again, and you judiciously retreat to the doorway of the closet. Keeping an eye on the chest, you swap your knife and the canister for your flare gun.

You point and shoot. The flare lights up the room, and whatever is in the chest freaks out. The box rocks and jumps, but the lid stays shut.

You put your fingers against your lips, tasting the sweet saltiness of your blood, and you say the final Word that sets the

Closing Ward. The flare glows bright, slaying all the shadows in the closet. The cedar chest ignites.

It smells nice as it burns.

Well, until the flames start burning the body inside.

Thankfully, you've already left the house by that time . . .

A NIGHT OFFICE FIELD OPERATIVE DOES WHAT NEEDS TO BE DONE. THEY DON'T SECOND-GUESS THEIR ACTIONS. THEY DON'T SPEND A LOT OF TIME REFLECTING ON THE CHOICES THEY MADE IN THE COURSE OF DOING THEIR JOBS. THERE ISN'T ENOUGH GIN IN ALL THE WORLD TO DEAL WITH THAT. SO PLAN ACCORDING.

ASSESSMENT SCORE: 81

Please refer to the Appendix for further information regarding your Assessment Score.

88

You can see a stone wall through intermittent gaps in the hedge. You're on one side of the maze—er, labyrinth. Whatever this thing is that you're stuck in. The wall makes you feel like you're not totally lost. *If this thing has one side, it has another,* you think. And if it has two sides, then it probably has a third and fourth. The third is where you and Archer came in. *Two out of four,* you think. *We're making progress.*

"To the left," you tell Archer.
Go to 117.

"Let's stick to this path," you tell Archer, indicating the route that will keep you parallel to the wall.
Go to 119.

89

This clearing is different than all the other clearings because it is where all the leaves went to die. They make piles of various and sizes. You plow through the piles, making lots of noise. You wonder if there is a dead body here somewhere. Not that you'd ever find it in all these leaves . . .

Archer falls behind. She's got that faraway look in her eye.

"What do you see?" you ask.

"It's nothing," she says. "Just a shadow."

"Oh, okay," you say. You don't give it another thought. Though, that may be a foolish decision . . .

Go to 112.

It's never just 'nothing,' you think. Not when you're on a job. "We should check it out," you say. "Just to be thorough."

Archer fidgets for awhile before she nods.

You take the righthand passage.

Go to 114.

90

The stairs creak as you go up, and you wonder how Pearson could have managed the stairs without you hearing him. The air gets colder as you ascend, and when you reach the landing, you can see your breath.

The landing includes a broad sitting area that probably looked out over the back yard, but all those windows are blocked over with plywood now. A set of French doors would have opened up onto a deck of some kind, but again, plywood keeps everything closed up tight.

The banister runs off to your left for a few feet, and there are a set of double doors that lead to the master bedroom. On your right is a narrow hall that leads to other rooms.

The flooring is the same here as it is downstairs: wooden and bare. In some places the wallpaper is streaked with dark stains, like something has leaked down from the attic.

There's a large pot near the hallway on your right. It might have held a fern or a small tree at one point, but all that remains is a dark mix of dirt and ash. You wonder if something is buried in the pot, like a family pet or something . . .

Start with the French doors.
Go to 111.

Check out the master bedroom.
Go to 113.

Check out the hall to your right.
Go to 116.

That pot looks suspicious.
Go to 118.

91

You approach the windows of the solarium. The drapes hang in strange folds, and as you are reaching out to touch one of the panels, you stop.

These aren't drapes. They're hanging strands of pale mushrooms, packed so tightly together that their caps nearly merge into a single sheet. You peer up, squinting at the ceiling. What you had mistaken for metal struts forming the framework for the solarium windows are actually thick roots. You marvel at the symmetry of their growth. *They feed off the metal*, you think. *It's not a natural arrangement. They grow where the food is.*

You shine your light at the strands of mushrooms, and the "curtains" ripple slightly, as if disturbed by the illumination. You shut the flashlight off and hold it down at your side. Holding your breath, you start inching back from the mushroom curtains. *Too close*, you realize. You were too close. You silently curse at your complacency. How did you get so dull-witted?

The rippling stops, and you let out the breath you had been holding.

Too late you realize what you've done. The strands of mushrooms directly in front of you light up. The light spreads like wildfire through all the strands, and in an instant, the whole room is ablaze with light. You raise an arm to shield your eyes and fail to see what happens next. By the time you notice, it's too late . . .

The mushrooms disintegrate, exploding into thousands and thousands of tiny spores. You backpedal, trying not to breathe, but your lungs scream out for air. You suck in a quick breath.

You clap a hand over your mouth and flee from the room. Maybe you got lucky. Maybe you didn't inhale any of the spores. Maybe you'll be okay.

But even before you get to the foyer, you know you won't.

They're in your throat. You can feel them, like shards of glass when you swallow. They're in your belly too, exploding when they come into contact with your stomach acids.

You stagger against the wall and slide to the floor. You should get up. You should keep moving. But you know there's no point. Your stomach is already ruptured. The spores are spreading.

You cough, and blood spatters on the back of your hand. Black spots swirl in your vision. You know some of them have gotten into your eyes.

You fumble in your coat for the squeeze bottle of holy water. Your hand is shaking as you raise it to your lips.

This is going to hurt.

You squeeze the plastic bottle. Something cold rushes into your mouth. For a brief moment, the pain is gone, but then it comes racing back.

"Too late," you croak. These are your last words . . .

SPORES WILL GET YOU EVERY TIME. THERE'S A NIGHT OFFICE ASSET RESOURCE MANAGEMENT WHITE PAPER ON HOW TO IDENTIFY AND AVOID THEM.

ASSESSMENT SCORE: 46

Please refer to the Appendix for further information regarding your Assessment Score.

92

Keeping close to the wall, you creep over to the hearth where solid stone gives an illusion of safety. When you look back at the floor, you swear you see it ripple slightly, and you're doubly glad you didn't go after your flashlight.

The hearth is wide, and you could crouch down and fit inside the actual fireplace. You hesitate, remembering when you nearly burned to death in that barn out near Covington. You had been able to draw a circle of protection with an old log before the flames reached you. Otherwise, you would have suffered badly.

Fire is such a terrible way to go . . .

You shake those memories off and focus on figuring out a way to get out of this room without touching the floor. It's probably impossible. You could try sticking to the edge of the room. That might work.

Or, you could try St. Herbert's Shuffling Step. It's only useful against creatures that are attracted to rudimentary rhythmic patterns. More highly evolved devourers won't fall for such simple tricks.

As you eclipse the beam from your flashlight, you notice a variation in the texture of the mantel. There's a patch of stone that has been worn smooth. When you run your fingers along it, there is a little give. You press harder and are rewarded with a noticeable click. A section of the bookcase next to the hearth jumps forward, revealing a dark gap.

A secret passage!

Boldly, you lean over and grab the edge of the bookcase. It swings easily, moving on a hidden hinge. The bookcase blocks your flashlight's beam, and you can't see much of the space behind the case, but it looks like a landing with a darker hole beyond it. Eventually, you make out the angled shape of a banister and you realize there are steps going down.

You don't recall anything about a basement in the notes on the house, but then, you really didn't read them that closely, did you?

It doesn't matter now. This is a way out.

Be brave. Leap into the unknown. (Don't forget your flight-light.)

Go to 115.

Basements are dark. Monsters hide in basements. This isn't necessarily the *better* option. You could go back. Or try to, at least.

Go to 120.

93

Pearson wanders in while you are contemplating the desk drawer. "Kitchen's clear," he says. You make some noise indicating you've heard him, and he comes over to the desk.

He's standing too close, and the miasma of funky body odor and stale tobacco wraps itself around you. It makes your skin crawl, a sensation you know better than to ignore.

You step away from him, putting your back to the wall. "Bottom drawer is locked," you say. "I need you to open it."

He looks at you, and you get that feeling—again—that something is off. There's a vibration around him that isn't right. You've learned to distinguish between the nervous energy an operative throws off during a job and a deeper twitch—that unconscious panic signal the psyche throws out.

You have your secrets too. It's an occupational hazard, in a way, and you learn how to live with it—both in what you read from others and what they read from you. Every operative knows that should the situation go off the rails, their first responsibility is their own self and sanity. The Night Office has lost too many over the years due to operatives trying too hard to be nice and kind to one other. *Do everyone a favor*, the Old Man used to say. *Save yourself.*

Pearson activates his Hand and puts it on the desk. The wood shivers, and every drawer pops open. It's a bit much, but Pearson's got some adrenaline to burn off.

You wonder what happened in the kitchen . . .

He reaches into the bottom drawer and pulls out a metal box. It looks like an old cash box—simple, with a latch a monkey could pick—and it jangles noisily when he drops it on the desk. Since he picked it up with his Hand, his Opener magic has already bled into the box. The lid pops open without anyone asking.

He turns slightly and reaches for whatever is in the box with his left hand.

Why is he using his left hand? Something's wrong here.
Go to 110.

You are highly strung at the moment. It won't look good on your report if you kill a member of the team for nothing more than being an asshole.
Go to 121.

94

You can't keep sprinkling salt on your partner. It's going to kill him too!

Swearing, you stop with the salt. You're going to have to try something else. You fumble with the many pockets of your jacket, trying to figure out what will be useful.

Ceremonial knife? No, you'll just be stabbing your partner—which, okay, wouldn't be terrible, but it might be fatal.

Holy water? Doesn't work on shoggoths. It's like trying to use butter to stop a fox from eating chickens.

Snuff powder made from the ground up finger bones of a saint? Shoggoths aren't intelligent enough to be threatened by old mystical nonsense like that.

Elder stone? Of course. An Elder stone always works. That's why they're handed out like candy corn by the armory staff. Now, where did you put that stone?

While you're fussing with your pockets, Pearson heaves himself to his feet. He collides with you, and you stumble back a few steps. He comes with you, and it's almost like you are dancing. Why is he pressing so close?

He's stuck to you. The front of his coat has turned into a black webbing that is snaring both of you.

You try to pull free, but Pearson gets a hand on your shoulder. You try to block his other arm as he goes for a hug, but blocking isn't going to help. It's still contact, and contact means more points where the shoggoth can bind you two together.

Damnit. This is what you get for being considerate.

Pearson pulls you close, almost as if he wants to hug you for your weakness. But this is a hug that isn't going to end well. You struggl to pull free, but the web is getting thicker somehow.

He leans in, and his mouth stretches wide. It's going to be the sloppiest of sloppy kisses. You turn your head, unwilling to meet him face-on. Something licks your cheek. Something rough, like a barbed tongue or a tentacle . . .

You hear a whimpering noise and realize it is coming from your throat.

This isn't the way you wanted to go. Not like this . . .

THERE'S NO NICE WAY TO PUT THIS, BUT YOU HAVE BEEN EATEN BY A SHOGGOTH WEARING A HUMAN SKIN-SUIT. THERE ARE ONLY ONE OR TWO WAYS TO DIE THAT ARE MORE HORRIBLE THAN THIS. WE HOPE YOU DON'T HAVE TO FIND OUT WHAT THOSE ARE, BECAUSE THIS IS BAD ENOUGH.

ASSESSMENT SCORE: 18

Please refer to the Appendix for further information regarding your Assessment Score.

95

You know better than to turn your back on what is obviously a trap. You Close the cedar chest so nothing can jump out at you while you're investigating the tub in the other room. The chest quivers slightly as your magic takes hold.

You go to the bathroom door and shine your flashlight over the large tub. It's deep, and yes, those feet are as taloned as you first thought.

The noise comes again. It's a squeaking scrape of leather against marble.

"I know you're in there," you say loudly for Pearson's benefit.

The noise don't come again. You notice your breath is misting from the chill in the air.

"Are you still Pearson?" you ask, not expecting an answer.

A throaty giggle rises from whatever is in the tub. The chill moves down your spine.

"I can hear him screaming," it whispers. "So small and tiny. So filled with fear."

"What do you want?" you ask, going against the rules outlined in all the manuals. Never negotiate with horrors from beyond.

"Blood and souls," the creature in the tub hisses.

This is partly why you don't bother negotiating. They're not very imaginative.

"Not today," you say. "In fact, I'd like the one you are wearing back."

"Can't have it," the monster says petulantly. "It is leaking." It giggles again.

You've heard enough. You feel around in your pockets for that jar of naphtha. When you shake it, the colors turn orange and red.

It's convenient that the monster decided to hide in the tub. Keeps things contained, doesn't it? You flick the jar with a fingernail, setting off the timer. You toss the jar into the tub, and then duck out of the doorway. There's a bright flash of light and the wall shakes as the naphtha ignites. The monster makes a drawn-out keening noise. Like a tea kettle or a sack of cats.

The tub took the brunt of the blast, but there are scattered streaks of fire on the walls. You let them burn. The whole house can go up, for all you or anyone else cares.

Your work here is done.

Pity about Pearson, though.

SOMETIMES YOUR PARTNER DOESN'T MAKE IT. THIS IS AN OCCUPATIONAL HAZARD. YOU WILL NOT PENALIZED FOR THEIR ERRORS OF JUDGMENT.

ASSESSMENT SCORE: 82

Please refer to the Appendix for further information regarding your Assessment Score.

96

You drum your fingers on the top of the desk while you wait for Pearson. After a few minutes, you decide it's just a desk drawer and it probably won't hurt you to open it without him. You snap the lock with the tip of your ceremonial knife.

There's nothing in the drawer but an old cash box. Inside the box is a leather journal, tied with rawhide. The leather is worn and cracked—the book is fifty or sixty years old, at least—and the edges of the pages are stained. There's a faint smell to the journal, like it was hand-cured by an eager amateur. The handwriting is neat and tidy, and you thumb through the pages.

The contents tell a pretty dark tale, filled with the worst sort of enthusiastic record keeping.

When you surface from reading, you realize you've lost track of time. *Where is that asshole?* you wonder. You slip the journal into one of the bigger pockets of your jacket and go look for your partner.

You don't find him in any of the rooms downstairs.

The dust on the floor in the foyer is no help. Both you and he have been back and forth so much the tracks are all messed up.

The hair on the back of your neck stands up. You raise your flashlight, shining the light up the stairs. You see a white face for a just a second, and then it is gone. Was that Pearson? You're not sure. And why did he run? No easy answer to that question either. *Too many questions.*

Head upstairs to the master bedroom.
Go to 76.

Check out the rest of the upstairs first.
Go to 79.

97

Pearson keeps banging his heels on the floor, and you feel the psychic gut punches of his Hand as he grabs at the shoggoth. It's trying to get away from your salt shaker, which means it's trying to force its way into his body.

His head slams back against the cabinet, and his eyes roll up in his head. His teeth grind together, and there's blood on his lip.

This isn't good. It's going in through his ears.

You upend the bottle over his head. His hair catches on fire, and he starts screaming. There's shoggoth scattered around him like crusty bits of old jelly, but you didn't get it all, did you? Some of it is inside his brain.

His cheeks shudder and his eyes roll back down. His pupils are enormous and he can't focus. He gasps like a fish out of water, and spittle flies from his lips. There's an acrid smell all of a sudden, and you realize he's pissed himself.

It's definitely in him. The shoggoth is rewiring his brain.

You are a Closer; you could seal it in him. But that doesn't turn out well for Pearson. So let's call that the worst case scenario, okay? Instead, how about some of the basic purging spells you learned as a first-year apprentice? There are ways to safely eject an extra-dimensional rider.

But that was a long time ago, back when you were young and eager to learn. Back when the Old Man was still around.

You smack Pearson on the forehead and hold his head against the cabinet. You try to remember the words. What were they? *Anaal-Nathrakh* . . . No, not *those* words. Those are summoning words.

Pearson grabs your wrist with his Hand, and his eyes snap into focus. They're dark and evil.

What's looking at you isn't Pearson any more.

Close him. It's a terrible thing to do to a human being, but he's not human anymore. You've got to cage that shoggoth before it can escape. There's nothing worse than a free-roaming shoggoth wearing a human skin-suit.

Go to 122.

Hold on. There might be a way to save him. Sure, he's a jerk. But no one deserves to die this way, right?

Go to 126.

98

Idle curiosity will kill you every time, the Old Man used to say. *You don't need to look on the face of evil. You don't need to stare into the Abyss. You just need to know that it is on the* other *side of the door you are Closing. Looking is what fools do.*

Curiosity is what makes you human, though. It's what makes you different from *them*. Blind obedience—*not* looking, *not* questioning—is what lead to the extinction of the Fhynyem, and what allowed the Pale Scourge to grow unchecked for twenty millennia.

So, yeah, you're going to look. But you're not going to be an idiot about it.

You back out of the closet as you dig in your coat pockets for some tools. First, you draw on the floor with your Sharpie, making a diagram that intercects with the threshold of the closet. Then you make a tiny pile of crystals that touch the frame of the closet door—contact is important.

Backing up a few more steps, you position yourself so you can see the chest in the closet. Satisfed of your distance and line of sight, you sprinkle salt and sulphur around you. Once you write the appropriate protection sigils on the floor with your Sharpie, the salt and sulphur ignite. It's a good circle. You're sealed in.

Only then do you say terrible things about Pearson's mother.

Not that you knew his mother; it's just the easiest way to get a lizard brain response from someone. If they've been compromised by an alien intelligence, there's usually not much higher brain left. You've got to hit them where genetic memory still lingers.

The chest wiggles as you talk shit about Pearson's family. You mention sex with barn animals—a little much, probably, but you're not about to go over there and rap your knuckles on the box to get his attention. Fortunately, it does the trick. The latch pops on the chest.

The top of chest unfolds in a way that isn't normal, and Pearson climbs out.

He actually climbs, like there's a ladder that goes somewhere far away. *It's a void portal,* you think, and your stomach knots itself. *They got him to open a doorway.*

His face is slack, like he's been sleeping too long and is having trouble waking up. His clothes are dirty, smudged with something dark and viscous. "Yoooooo," he says slowly.

"Yeah, it's me. Why'd you let them take you, Pearson?"

You don't expect an answer. What was Pearson is long gone. You wonder how it got to him, and the answer comes fairly readily: *it wasn't one touch, but many.* Everything bent about this place took a bite out of his mental armor. You've been under the same assault, of course, but for whatever reason, you were less susceptible to it all. Less naive. More cynical. More experienced. Who knows? It doesn't matter, in the end. That's the way it is with the Night Office. No one expects to live forever.

"Cooommming throooo," Pearson says, flopping a boneless arm at the open chest behind him.

"Not yet, they aren't," you say. But the monster's words sent a chill up your spine. You don't have much time.

Set off your Closing trap now!
Go to 123.

Patience is a virtue and all, right? Do you have what it takes to wait a little longer?
Go to 124.

99

You shine your flashlight around the library until you spot the thing in the corner. It hisses at you when you shine the light on it, but it doesn't flee like the others. It crouches on all fours, more goat-like than human, and its face is misshapen with too many teeth and too many eyes. It says something, but you don't understand it because it has just too many damn teeth its mouth.

Not that you were going to have a long conversation anyway.

You grab the vial of holy water from your jacket, as well as the greenish soapstone that every Closer carries. The monster hisses again when you show it the Elder Sign.

You uncap the vial of holy water, and flick some of it at the monster. It shrieks as drops touch its wrinkled skin. Deep within its animal brain, it makes a decision. It charges at you, which is exactly what you were hoping it would do. You flick more holy water and keep the Elder Sign pointed at it, which only serves to increase the monster's agitation.

As you are about to say the words that will grab the beastie and turn it into a pretzel, someone taps you on the shoulder.

"What the hell?"

You realize as soon as you look that you've been tricked.

It'll be one of your teammates. It doesn't matter which one. It might even be someone else entirely. Regardless, it's an illusion. A distraction from what is front of you.

It's one of things the Old Man harped on about. *You don't interrupt another operative,* he would shout during training. *Distractions are death. Not just for you, but for everyone in the room.*

The monster is on you—*in* you. You can feel it in your brain. You've lost track of what is real and what isn't, haven't you?

The monster giggles, its breath is hot in your ear. You can

feel a laugh bubbling up from your belly. *There's nothing funny about this*, a part of you thinks. A part that is getting smaller all the time. *It's such a long way down*, this part thinks next.

And then even that part disappears into the Abyss and you cease to exist . . .

ALL THEY HAVE TO DO IS DISTRACT YOU ONCE . . .

ASSESSMENT SCORE: 39

Please refer to the Appendix for further information regarding your Assessment Score.

100

As you move down the hall, you note that the door at the end of the hall is fully closed, while the door on your immediate left is *mostly* closed. You get the sense that you are being led, and you pause for a minute.

Something has gotten into Pearson's brain. Maybe it started when he looked in the hall closet; maybe it got into him somewhere else in the house. Regardless, it's eating his mind. How much of Pearson is left, and how much of that body is being driven by spectral intelligences from beyond Tau Ceti?

You don't know for certain, but your gut sense is that the door at the end of the hall is booby-trapped. When you trip that trap, Peason is going to jump out at you from this room on the left.

Well, there's no reason to be predictable, is there?

You find the grey marbles in your jacket. You roll them around in the palm of your hand until they're warm. When they start to steam, you roll them down the hall.

The marbles aren't on the Night Office approved list of field assets. Mostly because they're parasitic. They feed off your aura and, when activated, broadcast psychic signals. *We're warm flesh sacks! Hot blood! Hot blood!*

These sorts of things are frowned upon, of course, but you don't tell the Night Office everything. They expect you to come home. The rest is all shades of plausible deniability, anyway.

The marbles roll down the hall and—one, two, three—they hit the far door. They trigger something, all right. The door explodes, transforming into a snarling mass of splinters. The cloud of wood barely covers half the distance to you before it is sucked back, drawn into a howling vortex in the far room.

A void mouth! Any closer, you'd have been sucked in.

The mouth collapses on itself, and in a second, there's nothing left of the door, or your marbles.

The room is empty now. It's sort of anti-climatic.

You look at the nearly closed door on your left. You wait.

Nothing happens.

Very quietly, you inch forward. You get your Sharpie out and hold it ready. When you are close enough to touch the door knob, you pause. You listen carefully.

After awhile, a floorboard squeaks, and that's all you need to know.

You grab the doorknob and yank the door shut. Holding the door closed, you scribble sigils along the panel where it touches the frame.

Something grabs the knob on the other side and pulls. You nearly lose our grip but you manage to hold on.

You finish the first Ward. You spit on the writing, activating it. Someone yelps from within the room. They just got burned. You smile grimly, and keep writing. You finish the second Ward as something heavy slams against the door.

This ward is going to need something stronger than spit. You bite your lip until it bleeds. The second Ward goes up with an audible crackle of power, and now you can let up on the door-knob.

"It's me." Pearson shouts from the room. "Let me out!" You ignore him, and start working on the third Ward. This one will take a few minutes. "Come on," Pearson pleads. "I know you can hear me."

You keep working. You're not saying a word until the third Ward is done.

He keeps at it, though after awhile, his pleading gives way to threats, When you are nearly done with the Ward, his voice changes. "I'm going to eat your soul," the creature inside of Pearson shrieks.

You finish the last part of the Ward. "You're going to have to open this door first," you say. You tap the door three times, leaving three dots.

The Ward of Persistent Intent. Dot.

The Ward of Elastic Separation. Dot.

The Ward of Eternal Closure. Dot.

You touch two fingers to your bloody lip, and then smear your signature through the dots.

The final Ward ignites, the symbols burning into the door. The material hardens.

Inside, Pearson rages, calling your all sorts of names. Making all sorts of threats. You listen to his invective for a minute or two. When he runs out of breath, you tap the cap of the Sharpie against the magically-hardened door panel. "I'm going now," you say. "But you can keep talking all you like. You've got an eternity . . ."

The house will be torn down in a few days. When the demolition crew tries to open this door, the entire corner of the building will compress itself into sub-atomic particles. If the Night Office wants to do something about the demon inside this oubliette between now and then, well, they can send out an extraction team.

Your work here is done.

YOU REMAINED CALM AND DID YOUR JOB. WELL DONE.

ASSESSMENT SCORE: 85

Please refer to the Appendix for further information regarding your Assessment Score.

101

Both the room on the left and the room at the end of the hall have doors, and both doors are hanging ajar, innocent as you please. It's hard to say which one is the bad choice, and so you root around in the many pockets of your coat for that flashbang grenade you dimly recall picking up awhile back.

Ah, there it is.

You twist the timer and roll it into the room at the end of the hall. It goes off with a burst of intense light and a cloud of thick smoke. You charge into the cloud with your flashlight in one hand and your ceremonial knife in the other. The smoke stings your eyes, but it dissipates quickly, revealing an empty room.

Pearson isn't here.

The door creaks behind you, and you whirl around.

There's something standing in the doorway. Something too pale and too slender to be human. It has teeth, though. Lots and lots of teeth. Its mouth looks like a shark and a lamprey had sex. The offspring has all the worst dental characteristics of its parents.

It fills the doorway, and when it braces its hands against the door frame, the building groans.

From somewhere behind it, Pearson starts yammering.

You can't hear what he's saying, but you can guess that he's congratulating himself for having led you into this trap.

The thing is: a trap only works if you can get it to close, and Pearson's an Opener . . .

The thing that Pearson has summoned is an over-teethed variant of a Yythian hunting sparrow. Like all sparrows, its bones are fragile, especially when you stretch them to something this size.

The thing chatters like a badly edited cut of a stop-animation movie. When you punch it in the chest, you hand goes right through its ribcage. If Pearson was half-clever, he would have hidden a second mouth in there. The damn thing is practically translucent, though. It's hard to hide a surprise in something you can see through.

You reach for the monster's spinal cord, and with a thought, you Close the gaps between the vertebrae. The monster's teeth chatter, but they're the only thing that it can move. With its spine fused, it's about as dangerous as a movie-tie in standee.

Pearson bolts. By the time you extricate your hand from the locked-up sparrow monster, he's thundered down the stairs. You give chase, only slowing down when you reach the foyer.

The front door is still shut, which means he didn't go out that way. You calm your breathing and listen. He panicked. He should be easy to track.

Ah, a creak from the library. That's where he's gone.

You enter the room cautiously, just in case he has another trick planned, but the room is empty.

There are bookcase built into the walls and a heavy hearth at the far end. One of the bookcases is hinged, and it is hanging open.

A secret passage!

You wonder how Pearson knew about it.

You shine your light through the opening and see stairs leading down to a basement. Was there mention of a basement in the operation notes? You skimmed them, so who knows if there was.

Doesn't matter now, does it? You're going to have to go down after him.

Seriously? This isn't over?
Go to 115.

102

The landscape slides sideways, and you experience a rush of vertigo. A trench opens beneath both of you. Archer grows wings, and you grab her ankle to keep from falling.

The black goat keeps growing limbs and a torso, but it's not a goat. It's human, though both male and female. Their body is covered with ritual tattoos, markings that make your head hurt when you look at them.

Archer produces a lantern from somewhere (wait? Aren't you the one with the jacket of infinite pockets?), and the black goat flees the light. You and Archer chase the strange figure as it dances through a field of red and orange pillars. You glance to the side, and see other figures. Some are following you; some are running in parallel.

Everyone is heading in the same direction.

You streak out of the pillars and find yourself on a broad plaza. There is a tall fountain at the end, and the fluid spewing from it shines like liquid mercury. The goat-headed person is making for the fountain, and as soon as you and Archer find your footing on the vaguely-unsettling stones of the plaza, you dash after them.

The goat person falls to their knees at the base of the fountain and raises their arms in desperate supplication. It keens in a voice that sounds like squirrels dying. Archer widens the shutter of her lantern, and the mercury drops of the fountain spark into ash.

Quickly, she shouts. *Before the ritual is complete.*

You reach for your ceremonial knife, but there is nothing left of it but the hilt. It was iron, and it didn't come with you into the Way. You search for something else. Something sharp—

And come up with your indispensable black permanent marker.

It's time to find out if the pen really is mightier than the sword.
Go to 125.

Force, as you know, is a great equalizer when it comes to blunt vs edged weapons. The end of the Sharpie is rounded, but it'll have to do.
Go to 168.

103

You recall your training about stepping into the Way. The one thing every operative is drilled on over and over again is how to pull yourself out. What's even better is that your entry into the Way was akin to a football team crashing through a paper barrier at a stadium. It doesn't take you long to find the shining rip you made. Grabbing Archer, you push yourself back through the tear in the spacetime continuum.

You fall through with a gasp. Your body is covered with a cold sweat. On the wall behind you, there are icicles hanging from the antlers on the stuffed deer head. Archer isn't far behind you, and when she fades back into this reality, you can see the strain on her face.

"It's okay," you say. "We're back."

"You . . . you should have warned me," she whispers.

"We saw enough," you say. "I didn't want to lock it in."

The Way isn't just the past and the future. It's also filled with what could be. Whatever you see in the Way is attracted by your awareness. These things drift toward you, and if you're not careful, they slip through the cracks before they seal. There are lots of horror stories about early travelers of the Way who unintentionally brought things back.

Archer's strength returns quickly. She steps close to the altar and peers at the head of the black goat. "It's a mask," she says.

You shine your flashlight at the rest of the heads on the wall. "They're all masks," you say.

Archer looks at you, her eyes wide. She's come to the same gruesome conclusion that you have. "Who is . . . ?"

You shake your head. "We don't need to know," you say.

"We do," she says firmly. "It's the key to the whole mystery."

You keep shaking your head. "We know," you say. "We saw enough in the Way. We know."

But Archer wants to be sure, and there is no dissuading her.

When Pearson joins you in the shed, you've managed to remove three of the masks. He looks at the mummified faces that have been revealed. "So that's what happened to Zelphepjer Sr," he says.

"Most of the family," you say, wearily indicating the other "stuffed" animal heads.

He points at the black goat head. "What about that one?" he asks.

"That one is real," Archer says.

The goat head leers at you. You can almost hear its braying laughter.

YOU'LL PROBABLY BE SCARRED FOR LIFE FROM THIS EXPERIENCE. THIS, TOO, IS AN OCCUPATIONAL HAZARD.

ASSESSMENT SCORE: 80

Please refer to the Appendix for further information regarding your Assessment Score.

104

It feels like you've been lost for an hour already, but it hasn't been that long really. The sky is starting to turn strange colors, though, which you take as a sign that you're going the right way.

Oh, and you are definitely in the Way. Archer hasn't said anything, but the sky doesn't start color-shifting like that on its own.

"Almost there," Archer says. She turns abruptly and squeezes through a narrow gap between two hedges. "What the—?" You almost don't follow her, but realize now is not the time to abandon your partner.

Go to 127.

"Can you feel it?" Archer asks.

"Oh, yeah, I can feel it," you say.

"We're almost there," she says.

You're not quite sure you want to know where there is, but it looks like it is just a little farther on . . .

Go to 131.

105

The front page of the journal says: "This record of my experiences belongs to Eliza Murray Zelphepjer. All of the acts described herein that I have done or that have been done to me are true. I do so swear."

Beneath is a smear of something on the page, and when you shine the light on it, you see the ridged impression of a thumbprint in dried blood.

You wonder what school taught Miss Eliza about "proper" journaling technique. There are a couple of candidates, and you know you could narrow it down when you got back to the Night Office.

You skim over the first few entries. They cover Miss Eliza's early sexual education, and read like a young school girl who has read too much Anaïs Nin and de Sade. It's not terribly original, and you roll your eyes slightly at how she signs each entry with a very gothic capital 'E.'

About two dozen pages in, she discovers sadism and blood rituals, and then things get a little grimmer. By the halfway point, she's tallying up the punishment she's meted out.

And then she writes about the Great Summoning Ritual, and that's when you stop reading. You know how this story goes.

Father doesn't know what we do, down in the basement. He doesn't know about the secret passage. He doesn't know about the room behind the furnace. He wouldn't understand. He isn't worthy . . .

You put the journal back in the metal box. It's a flimsy box, but it will have to do. You get the vial of sulphur flakes from one of the many pockets in your jacket, along with the mercury drops and the iron shavings. You sprinkle, drop, and dose the journal with all three ingredients. You get out your flint, and saying the right words in the right order, you strike sparks over the journal. When the sulphur flakes ignite, you slap the lid of the box closed and put your hand flat on top. The metal gets hot, but you don't flinch. When you say the Closing words, there is a flash of light and heat inside the box, and then white smoke drifts out of the ill-fitted seams.

One less story about a girl's seduction to evil in the world. It's a small step, but it's a step nonetheless.

You get up from the desk and go look for the secret passage to the basement. Miss Eliza gave you a clue in her journal. *All my secrets are hidden among the books*, she said.

Ah, a secret passage. You know where that must be.
Go to 136.

You have an idea about what she means, but you'd rather not rush into something that might be a trap. Haunted houses are tricky, after all.
Go to 129.

106

There's a stone pool in the center of this clearing, and it probably had fish in it once upon a time. You glance in, and see nothing but crusts of muck and a couple of skeletal remains. Scavengers that fell in and were too clumsy to get back out.

You shake your head. You're not a fan of starvation. That's a bad way to go.

Archer wanders widdershins around the pool, like she's a radio operator who can't quite find the signal she is searching for. "I keep hearing an echo," she says. "A woman's voice. It's here somewhere."

"Let's keep moving," you say.
Go to 89.

"This way," you say. It's an arbitrary choice, but if you let her, she'll keep circling the pond for hours. That's what happens when you get stuck in the Way.
Go to 109.

107

Now, who in their right mind finds a vital clue to the history of the house and decides to read it later? Wow. The Old Man would be really disappointed in you. It's a good thing he's dead.

Oh, right. The journal was what you were after all along, but you didn't consciously realize that, did you? No, you've been under the subtle influence of a vast cosmic intelligence since you crawled into this house. That's why you never noticed the body of your partner in the corner of that alcove down on the first floor. Nor all the blood.

None of that matters, really. You're going to dawdle as you file your report, and by the time it gets in the system, the house will already be demolished. There won't be any evidence left. Your report will be the final record, which means the terrible history of what went on in that house will never be known.

You're feeling pretty smug about all this as you drive home. The journal is safe in one of the many hidden pockets in your jacket. Along with Pearson's right thumb. What? So you took a souvenir. He's not going to miss it. Besides, Mr. Fish likes fleshy things to gnaw on.

Though, when you get to your apartment, you can't find him. You check all his usual hiding places, but he's not in any of them. "Come on, you little bast—"

You catch yourself. It's not like you to be angry with him. For a moment, you pause.

What's this? Why are you sweating all of a sudden? And why is your apartment so warm? It's old and very expensive to heat. That's why you normally wear an extra sweater. And Mr. Fish doesn't like the heat either.

Something hisses at you. Mr. Fish is crouched on top of the china hutch in the breakfast nook. What is he doing up there? Oh, he doesn't like you now. He knows what you did.

You slide open the drawer where the knives are kept. "Here, kitty, kitty," you say softly as you fumble for a knife. "Everything's okay. Everything is going to be all right."

Mr. Fish hisses at you again.

Kill it, a part of you thinks. A part you didn't know was there, but which is getting louder all the time. *Isn't it the very sort of creature you're supposed to be culling? Are you so weak you can't do what needs to be done?*

Your hand tightens on a knife.

You don't want to disappoint your new master . . .

A RESPONSE TEAM IS ON THE WAY. REMAIN CALM. THEY'LL TAKE OF EVERYTHING. DON'T WORRY.

ASSESSMENT SCORE: 38

Please refer to the Appendix for further information regarding your Assessment Score.

108

"This is like a bad trip on the merry-go-round," you tell Archer as you stagger into yet another clearing that looks just like the other ones. "It keeps going, and we can't get off."

"We're almost there," Archer says.

"How can you be so sure?" you ask.

"We're almost there," she repeats.

"You have no idea where we are going," you argue. "You're just saying that because you don't know what else to say."

Go to 132.

"Lead on," you say, indicating the nearest path out of the clearing.

Go to 137.

109

Something has been nagging you for awhile. "Are we always supposed to go to the right or the left in a labyrinth?" you ask.

"To the left," Archer says. "But this isn't a labyrinth."

You stop dead in the center of the clearing. "I thought it was," you say.

"There's no reason to believe it is," she says.

"But we've been keeping to the left, haven't we?"

"I'm—I'm not sure," she says.

"I thought you were keeping track?"

A look of mild panic crosses her face. "Was I?"

"What's the point of having you along if you're not keeping track of the Way?" You say it more forcefully than you mean, and you immediately regret your tone. "I'm sorry," you try.

She waves you off. "You're right," she says. "I should have been keeping better track."

"We should go this way," Archer says. She says it with some authority, as if she is trying to get everything back on track. You nod and follow her.

Go to 133.

"We can start now, okay?" You say.

She offers you a brave smile. "Okay."

You point at the lefthand passage. "Keep to the left, correct?"

Go to 137.

110

He's not using his Hand to reach into the box, which means one of two things: 1) whatever is in the box isn't sealed, or 2) he needs the Hand for something else.

If the reason is the former, then he's sloppy; if it is the latter, then you are the one being sloppy. Time to choose, Closer. What's it going to be?

If you have to think about it, you're already dead, you hear the Old Man say in your head.

And so you don't think about it. Your hand darts into your jacket and out again, flinging your ceremonial knife.

Pearson sees your movment and he brings his Hand up. The metal caps on his fingers are glowing. He's not quick enough though, and he misses his grab. Sparks fly—this is cold-forged iron, after all—and your knife hits him in the throat. He coughs and gurgles.

You grab the two-shot Derringer next. It's a close-quarters weapon. It's not something sanctioned by the Night Office, but you carry it anyway. Sometimes you can't help but get close. The gun pops in your hand, and two small holes appear in Pearson's forehead.

He flops back, landing on the desk, and then slowly slides to the floor. The glow on his fingertips fades, along with the light in his eyes.

Only after you verify that he is dead do you look in the box.

The only contents of the box are a leather journal. It's bound with a copper clasp. You pick it up gingerly. It looks old and feels older. A quick flick of the lock opens it, and you let the book flop open in your hand. The pages turn lazily, and you scan the neat handwriting.

Someone lived a very naughty life, more so since they wrote it all down. Some of what you read makes your blood heat up.

You've seen enough. You snap the book closed, and tuck it away in one of the deep pockets of your jacket.

You understand Pearson's agitation now, which makes the decision to go for your knife the right one.

Gold star, you think to yourself.

You leave the study. Since there's nothing else in the house, you leave it too.

Archer is waiting for you on the front lawn. "And?" she asks.

"Several generations of sex and violence, all wrapped up in some pretty terrible ritual messaging."

"Gross," she says. "Where's Pearson?"

"He was a fan of that sort of thing."

"Ew, grosser."

You look at her in the moonlight. Her hair is shining, and her cheeks are rosy. Like she has been involved in some strenuous activity. "Anything interesting in the back yard?" you ask.

"Pit of vipers," she says. "Though they may have been a psychosis-induced hallucination."

"It happens," I say.

"Yeah, it does." She shifts her shoulders. "The black goats of Uhr, though? They were definitely real."

"Black goats? Wow."

"And a hedge maze."

You shake your head. "You get all the cool stuff."

IT'S NOT ALWAYS GLAMOROUS, AND MORE OFTEN THAN NOT, SOMEONE ON THE TEAM DIES, BUT NO ONE EVER COMPLAINS THAT IT ISN'T INTERESTING.

ASSESSMENT SCORE: 66

Please refer to the Appendix for further information regarding your Assessment Score.

III

The plywood on the French doors is in the frame, and the doors themselves are locked with a chain and padlock. You might not be an Opener, but you still know how to work a pick. You slide a pair out of the hidden sleeve in your jacket collar and go to work. The lock is easy and you get it open without any trouble.

The doors are warped and stuck in their frames. You have to tug one hard to get it open, but it does open. The night air rushes in, and you inhale deeply. You've missed the night air.

You wander out onto the broad deck that extends from the back of the house. The deck sits on top of a covered porch. When you get to the railing, you look out over the yard. There's an overgrown lawn on your left, what looks like a hedge maze at the back of the lot, and on the right, there's the—

Well, it looks like a pool, but it is filled with a mass of bramble and thorns. Caught in the bramble is a small figure, dressed in black. Her pale face is turned toward the moon, and her white hair is spread out on the brambles. It's like someone got their fairy tales all mixed up, and instead of surrounding the castle with thorns, they ran them through the princess instead.

"Shit," you say, recognizing the figure.

It's Archer.

That's in. Enough of this. Call in the cavalry.
Go to 128.

This will not stand. You will avenge her, won't you?
Go to 138.

112

You've been going round and round in the hedge maze for what feels like hours. You and Archer are like the mythological serpent that eats its own tail.

When you get to the next clearing, you wave at her to stop. "What are we doing?" you ask.

"We're looking for Eliza Zelphepjer," she says.

"Who?'

She wrinkles her nose. "I didn't tell you?"

"No," you say. "I don't think you did."

"She's the source of the disturbance here," Archer says. "Spoiled rich girl. Bored. Got into drugs." She waves a hand. "The usual rebellion. You know how that goes."

"Too well," you say.

"I've seen bits and pieces of it in the Way. She met a man with ties to some esoteric group. Eastern European, I think. He was in the States as a visiting scholar, and she found his nihilistic philosophy very thrilling. Once she was under his thrall, he asked her to do . . . some dangerous things."

"She needed to prove her devotion to his cause?"

"Exactly."

"Strangling kittens?"

Archer shakes her head. "That came later."

She tells you more, but it all sounds the same and you tune it out. You're already exhausted, and the sordid story of Eliza Zelphepjer isn't helping. "Let me guess"—you say at some point, breaking into Archer's narrative—"eventually, he revealed he knew incredible secrets, but he's was lacking crucial funding to make it happen."

"Pretty much," Archer says.

"God, I hate bored socialites," you say.

Archer gives you that 'pot calling the kettle' look.

You ignore her. That was a long time ago, and unlike other stupid girls with too much time and money and not enough empathy, you found a calling. You found something worth saving . . .

"We should keep moving," you say.
Go to 86.

"What happened to the scholar?" you ask.
Go to 165.

113

You go into the master bedroom. There's a small bathroom and a walk-in closet at one end. On the far wall, where the bed went, there are mysterious stains. Like crime scene stains, but not so dark that you think anyone actually died in this room. Elsewhere in the house, sure, but probably not in this room.

There's an old cast-iron tub in the bathroom that looks like it had been used for target practice. You couldn't even fill it halfway with water before it would start leaking. There's no mirror over the sink, but you can see where one used to hang.

Just as well, you think. You don't need to see a reflection. You know how tightly wound you are right now.

There's a metal footlocker in the walk-in closet. Incongruously out of place, but that doesn't alarm you overmuch. This isn't your first operation. You know how reality starts to get slippery when an Opener and Closer are in play.

Something's in this chest, though; something that doesn't belong in this world.

You don't care what it is, really. It doesn't belong here.
Go to 135.

Yes, but shouldn't you look before you blast it into nothinginess?
Go to 98.

114

There's a pit in the center of this clearing, and in the pit are many spikes.

"Who puts a spike trap in their backyard hedge maze?" Archer asks.

"The home defense nuts," you say.

"Yes, but you'd think it would be in front of the house," she points out.

"True," you say. You check the hedges for a gap or something that would indicate there is a route out of this clearing.

"Look," you say. "There's a gap."
Go to 109.

"Let's go back and try a different route," you said.
Go to 60.

115

You stand at the top of the stairs that descend into the basement and play your light down the steps. They're old, but look to be in fairly good shape. You probably won't break through one as you go down. You notice there is less dust on the stairs than you've seen in the other rooms.

Taking a deep breath, you start down. Seven steps down, you stop and crouch, shining your light into the room below.

This the problem with an open staircase like this. Your feet are exposed for a long time before your arms and head. If someone were waiting to pounce on you, they would have lots of time to prepare before you saw them.

Someone like Pearson, for instance.

This isn't the first time you've been on an operation that has gone off the rails. There was that expedition to find that abandoned train out in Pennsylvania, for instance. That got really bonkers, but it was hours into the operation before someone lost their mind. You and Pearson have only been in the Zelphepjer house for what? A few hours? You would think Night Office operatives would be more stable than that.

Maybe the rumors are true, you think. Now that the Old Man is gone, there is less oversight. Budgets are getting cut. Operatives are being put back out in the field too quickly. They don't get the time they really need to shore up the cracks.

Not everyone has the comforting security of something like Mr. Fish at home. You've never been much of a people person, and Mr. Fish is just an convenient excuse to become even more of a misanthrope than you were.

The basement is surprisingly well finished. There's wood paneling on the walls. The floors are covered with the same stuff as upstairs. Off to the right, there's an oak bar with open cabinets and a mirror hanging behind it.

Large frames hang on the wall. They look like mid-century posters—maybe for movies or travel destinations. When you get to the bottom of the stairs, you see there is another room beyond the bar.

Check out the back room.
Go to 130.

Investigate the bar first.
Go to 139.

116

The hall leads to a trio of small bedrooms. In the one farthest from the landing, you find a thin series of wires hanging from the ceiling. It is the remnants of an old mobile, the sort one would hang over a crib. There's no crib here now, but the floor under the mobile is stained.

You can imagine what might have happened in here, but you'd rather not. It didn't end well for someone.

In the second bedroom, there is a square panel in the ceiling of the closet that leads to an attic. You shine your flashlight at the panel for a long time.

It isn't flush with the ceiling.

Oh, that loosened panel is going to bug you, isn't it?
Go to 142.

Since you don't have a step ladder in one of your pockets, it'll be tricky to poke your head up there. And that's a problem, isn't it? Because your'e not about to go play *Get 'em Gopher!* with whatever is up there, are you?
Go to 145.

117

"I really feel like we are going in circles," you say.

Archer stops. Her face is drawn, and her eyes are on the verge of being frantic.

"We *are* going in circles," you say. "Shit."

Executive decision time. Archer is no shape to lead. So, uh, make a random choice about which passage to take. Can't be worse than following Archer's lead, right?

Go to 146.

"This way," you say. "It's definitely this way."

Go to 137.

118

The pot is heavier than it looks, and you have to crouch down to shift it. You can rock it a bit, but tipping it over is going to take some work.

There's a dry smell coming off the dirt and ash, like it's been undisturbed for a long time. Suddenly, moving the pot seems like a really bad idea.

That's right. It's a bad idea. Let's leave it alone.
Go to 116.

Never leave things behind you that could turn out to be traps. Tip that pot over. Put your back into it, for crying out loud.
Go to 140.

Yeah, but . . . you can't ignore it, can you? Even though you should . . .
Go to 141.

119

The stone wall is still on your right. This is very comforting. "We're making good headway," you say.

Archer isn't as sure. "I feel like we are taking the long way around," she says.

"Well, I'm happy to take a shortcut if you know one or two."

She stops in the clearing. "There are no shortcuts," she says. "They always cost too much."

You suppress the shiver that wants to work its way up your back.

"Wait," Archer says. She turns toward the righthand passage. "I hear something."

You aren't attuned the way she is, but you're happy to take her word for it.

Go to 137.

"Okay, you say, "Let's not get seduced by that idea, then."
Go to 143.

120

It's been a long time since you practiced St. Herbert's Shuffling Step, an oversight you can kick yourself about later, if you survive. Right now, you need to remember how to do it and do it *well*, because whatever is under this floor is waiting for you.

Start with St. Herbert's mantras against fear. You remember those, at least. When you feel like you've got your heart rate under control, you mentally measure the distance between the hearth and the door. Before you overthink your calculation, you leap off the hearth and dash across the floor.

Well, it's more like a herky-jerky marionette dance as if the puppeteer were getting tased. Your teeth rattle as you jerk and stop and weave and roll. You sense the floor warping and rolling behind you, and every time you feel like it is going to warp in front of you, you flap to the right or jack to the left.

Keep moving. The Old Man is in your head again. *Never stop twitching.*

He was a good cheerleader when you were all learning how to stay alive. He wasn't one of those instrucors who believed in tearing his students down in order to remake them in the proper way. He believed you already knew who you were—and you had to know, frankly, otherwise you never would have wandered in to the Night Office's recruiting center.

The door is close. Just a few more steps. You can make it.

The space in front of the door crumbles and vanishes, but you were expecting this. Your last step is a leap, and you clear the hole easily.

You sprawl in the foyer, clear of the library with the warping floor. You lay still for a few minutes, catching your breath. Listening to the house.

You look behind you, and all you can see in the library is your flashlight, still lying by the bookcase.

As if you were fool enough to go back for it.
You lift your eyes to the staircase in front of you.

Time to head upstairs and finish the job.
Go to 90.

On the other hand, a responsible retreat while you are still sane is a perfectly solid plan.
Go to 64.

121

Pearson twists and shudders like he is having a seizure. You start to back away, but then he pivots and thrusts his Hand at you. What is he doing? You're out of reach. He can't grab you. His magic can't—

Something comes undone in your belly.

Your knees give out, and you collapse to the floor.

How . . . How is this possible? Your hands fly to your stomach. Inside your body, your guts are coming unraveled. *This can't be happening*, you think. *It's just an illusion.*

But what if it isn't?

Pearson watches you struggle to get your thoughts in order. There's a glint in his eye that doesn't bode well for you.

He must have cast an Opening on you. It lost power as it crossed open air, but it still had enough juice to wreck some of the cellular integrity of your intestinal lining. You're leaking on the inside. You have to repair the damage. You have to Close—

Pearson comes over and kicks you in the belly. Something pops inside you. It's hard to breathe, and your vision is peppered with swirling trails of burning stars.

"I never liked you," Pearson says. He licks his lower lip. "You were always watching. Always judging me. You Closers are always judging the rest of us."

You gasp, trying to draw enough breath to speak. You want to tell him that you aren't like that. It's just how the job shapes you. It makes you see things as broken, as needing to be fixed. All you ever wanted was—

"You're all terrible liars," he says. He flexes his Hand, and the etheric discharge at his fingertips makes dull popping noises.

You're lying on your side now, feeling like a fish out of water. Your mouth moves, but you can't make any words. You can't do what you need to do.

He reaches for your head. *Pop. Pop.* The metal tips of his fingers make firework noises.

You see more light. It's streaming in from everywhere, and a loud rushing noise fills your ears.

Pop. Pop. And then all of you comes apart . . .

ACCORDING TO AN INFORMAL SURVEY OF NIGHT OFFICE FIELD AGENTS, THIS IS, SUPPOSEDLY, A RATHER PAINFUL WAY TO DIE.

ASSESSMENT SCORE: 41

Please refer to the Appendix for further
information regarding your Assessment Score.

122

Quick as a whip, you snatch your ceremonial dagger out from under your jacket. Pearson's lips are moving, and spittle is dripping from his mouth. The thing in his brain doesn't quite know how to make the Hand work yet. There's still time.

This is why the Old Man taught you how to use the knife with either hand. *Some day you're going to have one hand shoved down the throat of some gibbering fiend*, he would say. *A good Closer can still perform their services with one hand. A great Closer can shut them out with just their feet. Surprise me, you shits. Show me that I'm training great Closers and not fresh meat.*

Pearson is still holding on to your other wrist, and your skin is starting to smoke. "I'm sorry," you whisper, but that's not the sentiment that powers the thrust with your left hand.

The knife goes in through Pearson's mouth. He chokes on a bubble of air, twitches once as the shoggoth tries to flee from the cold iron of your blade, and then his entire body goes slack.

His grip eases, and you pull your hand free. There are burn marks on your wrist. Those will heal.

You leave the knife stuck in Pearson's mouth, which is the best way to ensure that both man and space jelly stay dead.

The freezer drawer of the refrigerator is still open. You stumble over to the quietly humming unit, and close the drawer. Then you Close the whole unit. Sealed forever. Nothing is going to come through this gateway.

Oh, man. You are invincible.
Go to 147.

Well, you should check the upstairs before you congratulate yourself too much.
Go to 134.

123

You decide not to wait for more eldritch monstrosities. One you can handle, and you think your makeshift implosion bomb will take care of a half dozen, but who knows how fast they're going to come through. Void portals are tricky things. They can be different sizes on either end.

The monster is close to the door of the walk-in closet. It sniffs the wooden frame, almost as if it senses the invisible barrier between you and it.

Come on, you think. Mentally imploring it to take that extra step. Hoping it can read your mind. You imagine yourself dressed up like a turkey. *Gobble, gobble*, you think. *Don't you want to eat me?*

It takes one more step, and that's all you needed.

With a word, you set off the latent instructions imbedded in the crystals. They sputter with light, and a coruscating web of power shocks into existence across the doorway.

The monster lets out a frightful howl, showing more teeth than the human head is supposed to have.

You grab the psychic leads on the web and tighten it. The house groans and flexes as you drag everything closer together.

The monster charges the web and bounces off. Of course it does, you are a professional, after all. Though, you do feel a headache coming on. You figure it can hit the web once or twice more before your determination falters. It won't take the monster long to force a hand through after that.

You squeeze your fingers together, making a fist. The walls of the walk-in closet jerk inward, reducing the area by half. The monster pounds its fists against the nearest wall. You see shadows flickering in the open crate. More are coming!

You squeeze harder, and the bedroom ceiling fractures. The closet is small enough now the monster can touch both walls.

It tries to hold them back, as the tentacled head of something truly ugly and alien pokes out of the crate.

You hug your fist to your chest and wrap your other hand around it, squeezing as hard as you can. You feel like you're going to pop a blood vessel in your brain. Can you Close them off before you have an aneurysm?

It's always like this, you know. Death or salvation. There's no middle ground with your job. You either succeed or you are dead. The only trick, really, is choosing how you die. And when, but only if you are really lucky.

You exhale fiercely, driving all the air out of your lungs. One more squeeze!

The web across the door lights up, a dazzling light show that leaves you blind. Or maybe it's—no, wait, that's it. You squeezed the room into nothingness. It's all gone. There's nothing more to see.

You did it. You Closed the portal.

You squished an eldritch lieutenant—maybe even a lesser Old One. That'll look good on your report.

YOU HAVE CONDUCTED YOURSELF IN A REASONABLY PROFESSIONAL MANNER. WELL DONE.

ASSESSMENT SCORE: 92

Please refer to the Appendix for further information regarding your Assessment Score.

124

"Are you going to wait for your pals, or do you think you can take me on your own?" You taunt the monster in the closet.

It growls as it comes toward the threshold of the walk-in closet. But it doesn't breach the threshold. It's not *that* stupid.

"This is the problem with grabbing the weak-minded ones," you say. "They're not great against the real players. You guys have never figured that out. Not in, I don't know, how many centuries have you been trying to get a foothold on this planet?"

The monster grows more teeth and gnashes them together. While it's a terrifying display, it's also dumb because all it does is shred the body's lips and cheeks. And now it looks like a crowd-scene zombie from some low-budget, direct-to-video horror film.

You roll your eyes. They are so predictable some times.

Shadows flicker in the chest. The box bulges as something with lots of tentacles pushes through the portal. It heaves itself out of the chest, spilling itself all over the floor.

"Oh boy," you say.

It's not so much a bunch of tentacles as it is one tentacle with a bunch of little tentacle stalks. Like cilia, except, you know, a meter long.

The thing that used to be Pearson is shoved aside by the giant tentacle. All its cilia start thrashing and grabbing at the walls of the closet. Shredding the plaster. Tearing at the boards underneath.

Your guts tighten. Your magic doesn't extend to the walls. You only Closed the doorway. The walls are nothing more than plaster, wood, and insulation. A behemoth of any size is going to go through the wall like it was tissue paper.

You start incanting, trying to extend your ward. The strands of your magic start spreading into the walls. You've got to weave this thing tight and squeeze it down. You know you can do it, but it's going to take a minute or two.

Which might be time you don't have . . .

This is why we don't taunt the other side, the specter of the Old Man says in your head. He's even got that "I told you so" tone. *They'll just bring a friend or two through, and these friends are always—always—much much bigger. There is never a time when a situation won't get worse because you taunted an eldritch horror.*

You hate it when he's right, even from beyond the grave.

A crack runs up the wall next to the closet door, and you whisper the words faster, even though you know that's a cause for disaster. You're going to forget one, or mispronounce something . . .

The wall breaks, and a loop of giant tentacle plops out into the master bedroom. Dozens of its attendant tentacles writhe and reach for you. Some of them recoil from the electric shock of your circle of protection. Others hang on, their slimy flesh smoking and burning from the circle's power.

Suddenly, you're the one who is about to get squeezed.

This wasn't how it was supposed to go, you think.

It never is, the Old Man whispers.

Your circle sparks. You can feel it weakening . . .

WELL, THAT WENT SIDEWAYS IN A HURRY. THIS IS WHY ONE SHOULDN'T MESS AROUND WHEN ONE IS DEALING WITH ELDRITCH SPACE JELLIES.

ASSESSMENT SCORE: 61

Please refer to the Appendix for further information regarding your Assessment Score.

125

You grab the goat person by one horn, and jam your pen into one of its eye sockets. Hot liquid gushes all over your hand. The goat person thrashes beneath you, wailing and bleating.

The sun sucks the light out of Archer's lantern. Her hair comes undone and flutters around her head like a failing sunset. The fountain gushes faster, spraying mercury everywhere.

Something ponderous lands on the plaza. The goat person goes into a fit, and you have no choice but to let go. One of its horns is liable to get stuck in you if you don't.

You don't want to look behind you, because you know you'll likely go mad if you do. But the urge is strong. Really strong.

The goat person's moaning becomes more rhythmic. It's finding a way to turn its pain into song. You should have stabbed it in the other eye too, but that moment has passed.

You hear slithering noises, and now you look. Yeah, there are tentacles. Lots of tentacles. It's got a really long neck, which takes time to move. When the monster finally turns its face toward you, you see its hundred eyes.

It's impossible to not look in at least one of them. What you see there will haunt you for the rest of your life, which, fortunately, won't be very long . . .

THIS IS THE 'DEATH BY TENTACLED MONSTROCITY' ENDING.

ASSESSMENT SCORE: 58

Please refer to the Appendix for further information regarding your Assessment Score.

126

You can hear the Old Man's voice in your head as you lock eyes with the thing in Pearson. *You can't win a staring match with the Abyss. You can't beg for mercy from something that doesn't understand humanity. You are going to be devoured in a painful and bloody fashion if you think you can talk your way out of a confrontation.*

Pearson's lips twist into a gross caricature of a smile. His teeth are black.

You punch him in the face. His head snaps back. The blow isn't going to slow the monster down—it doesn't feel pain, remember?—and all you get is a brief flicker of satisfaction. You've been wanting to punch him for a few hours now.

Of course, that doesn't solve your immediate problem.

Pearson's grip is still tight on your wrist, and the fabric of your jacket is starting to smoke. The thing in Pearson is figuring out how to make the Hand work. In another few seconds, it's going to Open your arm, and that's going to be a mess.

You twist your wrist, pulling your arm back. He has to lean forward if he wants to hang on to you. Quick as a swallow in flight, you grab the push dagger you keep on the off-side of your jacket. It's good to have something sharp in easy reach. You stab him quick—throat, throat, eye.

Oh, he feels that.

While he's roaring, you pull your arm again, getting him to expose his wrist. You slash through the leather ties of the Hand. When you yank again, the leather glove slides off. The power of the Hand dissipates.

You back off a few steps. Pearson remains next to the cabinets. Black ichor is gurgling from his throat, and his right eye is a weeping mess, like a giant blister that's been popped. He is breathing hard, and snot is blowing from his nose.

"Come on," you say.

With a roar, he scrambles at you. He's terribly slow, and you sidestep him easily. You grab his collar as he passes and slam him into the refrigerator. His head bounces off the front, and when he slips, you shove him down, getting his head and shoulders into the freezer drawer.

He waves his hands, but you're behind him now, bracing your foot on the freezer drawer. He's half-in, and all the black stuff coming out of his wounds is pooling in the bottom of the drawer. The shoggoth is leaving his body, and in a minute or two, you're going to have to fight it again.

You start incanting. It's not a perfect seal, and that makes your job harder. It's not impossible to Close a door that is stuck. You keep pushing on the drawer, the muscles in your legs shaking from your effort.

Pearson gets more frantic. You speed up, speaking the words faster. The temperature in the room falls a few degrees. A rime of ice crawls across the front of the refrigerator, highlighting Pearson's bloody handprint.

You shove once more, and the drawer snaps shut with an audible click. Like teeth snapping together.

The bottom half of Pearson sags to the floor. The rest of him is inside the freezer compartment, along with the shoggoth. Pearson's left foot twitches. The blood from his lower half makes a large pool on the floor. It's already starting to crystalize. More ice crawls across the refrigerator.

Your Closing Ritual worked.

And why wouldn't it? There was a lot of blood to draw heat from. There's nothing in the literature that says it has to be *your* blood that is used for the sacrifice . . .

Ugh. You need to go throw up somewhere.
Go to 149.

You can puke late. Clear the upstairs first.
Go to 134.

127

You chase after Archer, and the branches of the hedge tear at your clothing as you push your way through the narrow space. The moon disappears behind a cloud as you try to extricate yourself from the hedge. You drop your flashlight. It rolls off somewhere, and you know you'll never find it.

You have some glowsticks in your jacket. You dig them out as you emerge from the hedge, your skin scraped and bleeding in a few places.

As it turns out, you don't need the glowsticks.

You've reached the center of the maze, and there is a large bonfire burning in the middle. Archer is standing between you and the fire. Her head is down and she is swaying from side to side.

You hang on to the glowsticks—just in case—and approach Archer.

Her eyes are closed. She looks like she is listening to music only she can hear. The fire is bright, but it isn't projecting any heat. In fact, when you stare at the flames, they flicker in and out of time.

"Archer?"

She doesn't seem to hear you.

You do, however, hear the voice coming from the fire. It slithers and whispers about how tasty human souls are. *Shiny, shiny,* it whispers. *So easy to snare. A little bit of what they've lost, and look how quickly they come!*

There's something behind the fire. Not here, with you in the maze, but somewhere else. Beyond this place. The fire is the bridge between here and there.

"What do you want?" you demand, even though you have a pretty good idea.

Supplication, it whispers.

"Fuck off," you say.

Naughty, naughty, it slithers. *I am going to eat this one if you don't behave.*

"Go ahead," you bluff. "She doesn't mean anything to me."

Such lies, it laughs. *Why else are you here?*

You don't have a good answer for that question.

It wants to play, you think. It feeds off panic and fear. It won't do anything to Archer as long as it thinks it can prolong your anguish. "You caught me," you say. "Yes, she means something to me, and if you hurt her, I will become very angry."

Anger is tasty, it whispers.

"You won't like the taste of my rage," you say. You lift one of the glowsticks and whisper to it. It starts to warm, and you snap it before the spell peaks. With a flick of your wrist, you throw it into the astral fire.

Something shrieks somewhere else.

"Let her go," you say. "Don't make me angry."

Archer starts to tremble, and spit foams on her lips.

You raise the other glowsticks. "Stop," you say. "It's been a long night, and I am not in the mood."

Privately, though, you wonder how far you dare go. Bluffing something that isn't human only works if it has a rudimentary emotional response system. Giving a shit about other creatures isn't high on the list of attributes you find in cosmic malignancies.

You never were very good at poker, but . . .
Go to 169.

Yeah, this bluff is going to go bad. Time for Plan B.
Go to 166.

128

"Enough of this," you say. You throw back your jacket so you can get at the long pocket in the back. You pull out the tube hidden there, and uncap the red-colored end. You sprinkle the powder in a wide circle on the deck, making sure the ward is well-marked on the dirty terrace. You uncap the yellow-coded end and draw out the magnesium flares. Using your Sharpie, you write on the ground inside the circle, spelling out in arcane letters what you need. When you're finished, you carefully step out of the circle of red dust.

The house can feel your anger and your intent, and in turn, you feel it start to formulate a response. *Too late*, you think as you pull the tab on the first flare. You turn and throw it through the open door, back into the house. Something gibbers and howls in there. There are dancing shadows mixed with the white sputter of the magnesium flare.

You pull the tab on the second one, and toss it into your circle. It burns bright, and then the red dust ignites. For an instant you can see your ward burning on your eyelids, brighter than the sun, and then the sky rips open. Everything gets very bright.

The house howls, but it's too late. The cavalry has arrived.

It occurs to you that—if you survive this inferno—you're going to be doing paperwork for about six months . . .

THIS IS THE DOWNSIDE OF HITTING THE PANIC BUTTON.

ASSESSMENT SCORE: 63

Please refer to the Appendix for further information regarding your Assessment Score.

129

You search the ground floor for some secret passage, and after an hour of finding nothing, you go upstairs. You know you're scraping the bottom of the idea barrel when you start looking for a dumbwaiter or a laundry chute or . . . anything that would get you underground. Ultimately, though, you have to admit defeat. If there is a basement, the entrance is hidden so well that finding it is way beyond your means.

This is why a team always includes someone who can see the Way. They can always find the secret passages.

And no sign of Pearson either. It's like the house swallowed him up, which is not a very enticing proposition.

Eventually, you end up back in the foyer, and as you are trying to figure out your next move, someone knocks on the front door.

It's an oddly normal sound, and it takes you a moment to place it. You eye the front door, wondering what sort of arcane trickery is going on. But whoever is outside knocks again, more forcefully this time.

"Hey, are you two dead or what?"

It's Archer, yelling from outside the house.

You try the latch and are surprised when it lifts. The door creaks open.

Archer looks like she's had a rough night. The sleeves of her coat are covered in ash and blood. Her face is bruised, and she's leaning against one of the porch supports like she needs some help staying upright. "You done yet?" she asks.

"I'm not sure," you reply. "I can't find Pearson."

"That's because I found him in the hedge maze out back."

"What?"

She shrugs. "Yeah. He was tangled up with something unspeakable. There was a void portal too. I could have used your help closing it, but . . ." She tries to shrug, but winces instead. "Anyway, that's all taken care of. Can we go now?"

You tell Archer about the journal. "Eliza Zelphepjer was a very bad girl."

"Yeah, no shit. Who do you think talked Pearson into opening that portal?"

"Wow," you say. "Undead succubus seduces a Night Office Opener and tries to open a gateway to the Bleak Beyond."

She rolls her eyes. "I know, right? Ugh. It's such a cliché any more."

You walk out of the house, pulling the door shut behind you. The latch clicks, but it doesn't sound like it is truly closed. "Hang on," you say.

You finish the job you came here to do.

THIS IS THE SORT OF ATTENTION TO DETAIL THAT THE NIGHT OFFICE LOOKS FOR IN ITS FIELD AGENTS.

ASSESSMENT SCORE: 84

Please refer to the Appendix for further information regarding your Assessment Score.

130

The back room is more of what you'd expect from a basement. There's an enormous furnace in the corner, along with several metal lockers for tools and other assorted junk that gets banished to the basement in suburban houses. Along the back wall, there's a hole in the cement floor, and a cheap wooden railing surrounds it. *Must be a well*, you think. One of those legacies of the last century that you don't see very often any more.

Off to your right, there's a pile of scrap wood and broken sheets of plaster. Construction leftovers. Probably been here since the last remodel was done on the house, not that you can recall those details from the briefing notes.

There's no sign of Pearson, and you've run out of rooms. He's got to be in here somewhere, unless you missed him upstairs.

Oh, man. Check the whole house? That sounds exhausting.
Go to 148.

Yeah, but space jellies can be crafty little bastards, so . . .
Go to 150.

131

There's an opening in the hedges up ahead. You feel a small thrill at finally finding the center of this fucking maze. Your pace picks up, but Archer grabs your arm. "Wait," she says.

You stop and shake your head. Damnit. You almost fell for it. The air is getting thicker, and there's a pressure behind your eyes. "There's something there," you say, which is like standing in the middle of a desert at noon and saying *Gee, it's a bit warm today, isn't it?*

Archer pats your arm and gives you a knowing smile. If anyone else gave you that attitude, you'd bite their head off. But it's Archer. She's got a light in her eyes that says she actually cares about you. You probably made her day by letting her save you from a horrible death right there, so that's good on you.

However, all interpersonal relationship nonsense aside, you still have to deal with the pulsating glob of eldritch malevolence waiting for you.

You and Archer approach the heart of the maze. The hedges peel back, revealing a gazebo. A pair of old oak trees flank the structure. It might have been white and terribly cute once, but time and the ichor from another place hasn't been kind to its faux gables and decorative trim.

Someone is waiting for you in the gazebo. She's mostly shadow, but you get a glimpse of a narrow face and fool-enticing lips. Her robe steams and squirms. You see a face here and there, swimming in the shadows. They're grinning mouths with lots of teeth.

"She's mostly shoggoth," Archer murmurs.

"I see that," you reply. You adjust your jacket as you approach, letting your fingers trip along the edges of a pocket or two.

Hello darlings, she purrs when you are within a dozen meters of the hellish gazebo. *I have been waiting.*

"We got lost a few times," you say, nodding toward the path behind you. "It would have been a lot easier if you met us at the pool."

She tilts her head, and something vaguely serpentine slithers around her neck and into the billowing shadows of her robe. *And let you chain me?*

You look at Archer. "We would have," you say.

"We would," she agrees.

The light is funny around the gazebo, a sure indicator that you are deep in the Way. Whatever is manifesting here had to coax you across a number of borders without you actively realizing it—or maybe Archer did. It doesn't matter, really—you're here now.

Archer catches your eye. She did her part. It's up to you now. You're the Closer.

You look at the malevolent figure. "What's it going to be?" you ask.

"Some sad and probably bullshit story about why we need to save you?"
Go to 164.

"Or are you going to give us the pitch about all the hot demonic action we can get if we sign on?"
Go to 167.

132

Archer whirls on you. "Fine," she snaps. "You lead, then."

You put up your hands. This isn't a fight you want to have right now. "It's just—"

You're not quite sure what you want to say. Yes, if the team has lost the Way, it's technically the fault of the operative who is supposed to be following the Way. But this is something you both know, so what's the point of saying it out loud? Archer is already upset. You can tell by the way she fidgets. Stay positive. Keep the focus.

"Look," you try. "We're here because you thought you felt something. I'm following you, but part of my job is keeping tabs on how far we go into the Way. I'm supposed to make sure we don't get lost."

"I'm not lost," she says, wrapping her arms around her waist.

"It seems like you are," you say. You try to be gentle with your words. "It's okay."

She wrestles for a minute and then relents. "Okay," she says.

"You're doing fine," you say. "Let's just take a minute and make sure we know where we are."

Archer turns in a slow circle, examining the clearing. "We've been here before," she says.

"Okay," you say. "That's progress."

"Not in this existence," she qualifies. "In another iteration."

"Well, that's not what I had hoped to hear next, but, okay."

"It's better than—" Archer starts, and when she doesn't continue, you get a little concerned.

"Archer?"

She looks stuck. Her pupils are dilated, and when you grab her hand, her fingers are cold. *Oh, shit.* Something grabbed her.

You let go before whatever it is that has snagged Archer in the Way can grab you too.

Shit, shit, shit.

You circle Archer, hoping that she'll come back. Like she was a radio station that suddenly went off the air. It's only temporary. She'll be back. But after a few minutes, you start to think that isn't the case. Archer's gone, and whatever snagged her has a hook into this place with her physical body.

You scrape the ground clear around her. You don't want to do this, but you have no choice. You dig around in your pockets until you find a garden trowel, and you use it to carve a circle in the dirt. You fill the trench with salt and sulphur, and you're about to set the Ward when you have a thought: your Elder Sign!

You dig out the greenish piece of soapstone and carefully approach your frozen teammate. Her gaze hasn't changed, and her skin has definitely paled. Using the edge of the trowel, you force her mouth open. Being careful to not touch her lips, you slip the Elder Sign in her mouth.

"I'm sorry," you whisper.

You prick your finger with your ceremonial knife and set the Ward. There's a flash of light from the circle as the Closing Ward ignites.

She starts to fade from view, no longer bound by this plane, and you stay there until she is gone. It's the least you can do.

SAYING GOOD-BYE IS HARD, BUT IT IS GOOD OF YOU TO BE SO DEDICATED.

ASSESSMENT SCORE: 72

Please refer to the Appendix for further information regarding your Assessment Score.

133

"This is a dead end," you say when you reach the end of the path. "There's no way through."

"What?" Archer peers at the dense wall in front of you. "I was sure this was the right path."

You tug at the nearest branch. "Not unless this is an illusion." The branch snaps back when you let go of it. "Nope. Feels pretty real."

"I was sure we were going the right way," Archer mutters.

"We should start over," you say.
Go to 58.

"Let's back up a bit and try that other path," you say.
Go to 137.

134

What happened in the kitchen leaves you feeling sick to your stomach, but you have a job to do. You've already swept the rest of the downstairs, and found nothing but dust and echoes of old pain.

Upstairs, there are several bedrooms, all of which have been stripped of furniture. In one of the smaller bedrooms, a wire frame of a mobile hangs from the ceiling. The floor is stained, and you'd rather not imagine what happened here.

There's a hatch in the ceiling of the master bedroom's closet. You Close it without bothering to check on how many dead bats are up in the attic. You've seen one bat graveyard, you've seen them all, really.

That's it, then. The house is cleared.

Back downstairs, the front door is still stuck, but it feels like it's more due to the weather than any malignant intent. You could break it down, but it's easier to knock out one of the plywood panels in the sitting room.

As you are climbing out the window, you sense someone standing in the yard. You tumble to the ground. When you struggle to your feet and assume a defensive stance, you recognize the person waiting for you.

"All clear?" Archer asks. Several strands of her pale hair are out of place, and there's a smear of blood across her forehead.

You lower your guard. "Yeah," you say. "All clear."

"Just you?"

"Just me."

She nods. You all mourn in your own way, but you've been trained to do it later. Finish the job. Get home. Those things always take priority. "Should we call a cleaning team?"

You shake your head. "Best to leave it all in place." You go stand with Archer and look back at the house.

"He was an asshole," she says. You're not sure if she's serious or if she's distancing herself from any emotional reaction she might have later.

"Well, he died the way he lived," you say, keeping it noncommittal. Just in case. You don't want to make things awkward right now.

"Good," she says. She looks at you. "You want to get a drink?"

"Sure," you say, striving to look nonchalant about the idea. You try to ignore the fact that your heart is beating faster than it did at any point during the job.

WHAT HAPPENS NEXT, CLOSER?

ASSESSMENT SCORE: 94

Please refer to the Appendix for further information regarding your Assessment Score.

135

You back out of the walk-in closet, until you are out of sight of the chest. Digging around in your pockets, you retrieve an adhesive patch and your Sharpie. The patch is store-bought. They come in packages of eight, and you only needed two after that weekend when things got a little out of hand around your apartment. You put a couple in your kit, because you never know what might come in handy when you're on a job.

You scribble a quick Ward. It won't hold long, but you don't need it to. When you're done drawing, you press the patch to your lips and breathe some magic into it. The patch goes rigid, and you work the corner of the backing until it comes loose.

Moving quickly, you go back into the closet. You strip off the backing from the patch and slap it across the latch of the chest. The magic triggers, and whatever is in the chest freaks out.

The chest leaps a half meter off the floor, and bounces and strains when it lands. Something huffs inside the chest, and you can imagine someone too big for the tiny space straining against a lid that won't budge.

"Pearson? Can you hear me?"

The chest stops thrashing, and you repeat your question.

Something growls inside the box. "There . . . Is . . . No . . . Pear . . . Son," it grumbles.

You totally hear "person," which—*ha ha*—is undoubtedly true, but such semantics are going to be lost on the rough intelligence inside the box.

"Can I get"—you pause and consider how specific you want to be—"can I get Pear-son back?"

"There . . . Is . . . Only—"

"Yeah, yeah," you interrupt. "I know this routine."

You glance at the patch. It's starting to smoke around the edges. It's not going to last much longer.

The monster in the box giggles again. It knows your magic is fraying too.

"Okay," you say. "Negotiating was fun, but talk time is over." You clap your hands and unspool a Closing web. It is shiny stuff, and it falls over the box like a baby blanket settling on a restless infant. The box thrashes under the netting. You ignore its efforts and tune the Closing. Tuck in a bit here. Pull that spot tighter over there. When it is all in place, you clap your hands again. The web shrinks to an infinitesimally dense point and then devours itself.

Some Closings are more dramatic and more permanent than others, which keeps the job interesting.

You'll have to file some paperwork about Pearson, but any summary judgement by Management will go in his file, not yours. You came back from the job, after all. He didn't.

ON THE ONE HAND, YOU SURVIVED. ON THE OTHER, SURVIVORS GET STUCK WITH ALL THE PAPERWORK.

ASSESSMENT SCORE: 87

Please refer to the Appendix for further information regarding your Assessment Score.

136

There is a secret staircase behind one of the bookcases next to the hearth in the library. It wasn't hard to find once you knew what you were looking for.

The chamber behind the bookcase is small, and the steps to the basement are steep and narrow. You shine your light down, and it's either a long way to the bottom, or there's a fog obscuring your light.

Neither of those choices plays well in your head. But down there is where you're going to earn that meager Night Office paycheck.

You dawdle for a minute, reflecting on what you read in the journal. Little Miss Gothic liked to have secret parties and she held them down in the basement, away from Daddy's watchful eye. She mentioned a hidden room behind the furnace where all the fun happened, and you guess that's where you'll find the greatest concentration of power. Pearson, too, if he's still ambulatory.

You wipe your hands on your pants, and then start down the stairs, taking your time.

Three steps down, you pass through the psychic equivalent of a thermocline. Nine steps down, everything is dark and spooky, but okay. Thirteen steps, there's a fuzz of white noise in your head. When you hit the fourteenth step, the mood darkens and your light falters. The air is heavier too, and something smells bed.

You still can't see the bottom of the stairs.

"Wonderful," you mutter.

The barrier was shielding the hot signal of all the energy zapping around down here, and maybe Archer would have sensed the foreboding atmosphere of the basement from the ground floor, but you had no idea.

You pause on the sixteenth step, seriously considering whether you should keep going.

You've got what it takes to finish this job!
Go to 152.

This calls for backup, you think.
Go to 156.

137

You are dizzy from all this walking in circles. How does it even happen? You haven't hit a dead end, and yet you feel like you're going round and round. "Archer," you call out. "This doesn't make any sense."

"I know," she says. "But we have to keep trying."

It doesn't even matter anymore, does it?
Go to 112.

"Trying" is starting to sound an awful lot like "Oh shit, I think we're lost."
Go to 117.

138

You don't have many friends at the Night Office. And Mr. Fish doesn't count. Which is why Archer's death hits you hard. She was kind to you on several occasions, and maybe that is the closest thing to friendship one has within the organization. There's a hollowness in your gut that you realize is a mix of sadness and resentment. She died alone.

No one should died alone. Not in this business. Though, it happens more often than not.

You wipe your face and glance up at the sky. It doesn't seem like it is raining, and yet . . .

Squaring your shoulders and adjusting your jacket, you head back into the house, determined to make some eldritch monstrosity pay for what happened to Archer.

Head for the master bedroom.
Go to 113.

Head for the smaller bedrooms.
Go to 116.

139

You stop at the bar and shine your light into the open cabinets where fine crystal was once shelved. You keep the light out of the mirror as you turn around. The back of the bar is empty too, except for . . .

There's a bottle tucked in the back corner.

You grab it and examine it in the light from your flashlight. Wiping off the dust reveals a pale label with sweeping yellow letters. Chateau d'Qyeure. 1962. It's some varietal of white. A Sauternes, in fact. Though, judging from the color of the wine, it's more apt to call it "dusky" than white.

You wonder if it is any good. You can't imagine that it is, or that you should even take it with you. God knows what sort of malignant spore is lurking in whatever ashy vinegar this wine has become.

Your hand shakes a little as you put the bottle back, and you know the influence in this house is starting to get to you. You need to finish the job soon, or you're going to end up like Pearson . . .

Oh, get on with it. Check out the back room.
Go to 130.

Hang on. Surely, the wine is still good, you think. *It can't be compromised.*
Go to 151.

140

You brace yourself and heave. The pot rocks on its base, but it doesn't go over. You shove it again—this thing weighs more than it should—and you get it almost over, but then it tips back again. It lands with a loud thud. The sound echoes throughout the house, and you pause for a minute. Did that echo go on too long?

You shine your flashlight around, making sure you're alone. You don't see anything. You put the light down and try the pot again. It's really heavy. What the hell?

Your hand slips, and the pot comes back down. Your foot is in the way, and the pot lands heavily on the end of your shoe, pinning to the floor.

That fucking hurts. You spend a few moments working through the pain. When the pain (and cursing) subside, you consider the situation.

You wiggle your foot in an attempt to extricate your shoe. It's not going to come easily. You're going to have to shift the pot. As you lean over to shove the heavy container, the top layer of dirt stirs. You freeze, barely daring to breathe, but then you realize what it was. It was just your own breath moving the dirt—all grunting and straining to move that pot. That's all it was. Nothing more.

You shift your weight a little lower, breathing out through your nose this time.

The dirt moves.

Oh, that wasn't you.

Vines shoot out from the dirt. They're black and covered with thorns. Before you can jerk your head back, they snake at you. They're trying to get in your mouth. Or up your nose. You grab the vines, and the thorns cut into your palms. More vines encircle your neck, and you feel the bite of the thorns as the vines tighten. More strands slither into your hair. A sharp pain blooms in your left ear as a vine wiggles into your ear canal.

Blood is running out of your nose now. The vines are pushing deeper, working their way toward the back of your nasal passages. You realize, with a mounting dread, that they're tunneling toward your brain . . .

YOU HAVE BEEN TURNED INTO PLANT FOOD. THEY'LL NEVER FIND YOUR BODY.

ASSESSMENT SCORE: 47

Please refer to the Appendix for further information regarding your Assessment Score.

141

Let's be cautious about this, shall we? If there is something in the pot, you don't want to be close to it. You put your back to the wall behind the pot. Bracing yourself, you put a foot against the pot and shove it.

The pot is heavier than it looks, but it does slide. Energized by your success, you keep pushing, and the pot slowly shifts towards the top of the stairs.

You take a moment to catch your breath. The pot is sitting halfway over that top step. You brace yourself and give it one last shove. The pot tilts. You hear a wild scrabbling noise, like claws on a parquet floor, as the pot goes over and tumbles down the stairs.

Halfway down, it shatters, scattering dirt and ash everywhere. There's something else too, something that uncurls as it slides down the stairs. You shine your light down, illuminating a writhing mass of dark vines. There are pale flowers too, buds that suddenly bloom with skeletal petals.

The pot monster orients on your light and starts hauling itself up the wooden staircase. It's coming for you, angry that you've destroyed its hiding place.

You reach into your coat and pull out the squeeze bottle of holy water. When the pot monster gets into range, you give it a generous squirt from the bottle. The monster shrieks—a psychic wail that makes your knees buckle—and it thrashes like a frog caught in a blender.

You give the bottle another squeeze. Several of the pale buds burst into flame. The monster keeps coming, though, and you keep squirting it as it tries to grab you with a whipping vine. But you stay out of its reach, and by the time the bottle is empty, the monster is nothing more than a burning bramble spinning down the stairs.

You put the squeeze bottle away. Everything is fine now.

Well, you know, except for all the weird shit that is happening. Everything in this house is coming alive and attacking you. That's not normal. Where is this influence coming from? How much blood was spilled here?

Head for the master bedroom.
Go to 113.

Let's do the rest of the floor first.
Go to 116.

142

Attic crawlspaces, especially in houses of this age and construction, are deathtraps. They're usually filled with exposed support beams, and many of them don't have finished floors. Line of sight is for shit, and you can't maneuver quickly if you need to.

Which begs a couple of questions: why are you even bothering with the attic? And how the hell are you going to even get up there?

There's no good answer to either of those questions, and after doing a mental inventory of what's left in your coat, you dig out a telescoping rod and an incendiary grenade. You extend the rod and poke the attic panel . It's loose, as you thought it would be, and with some judicious prodding, you get the panel moved out of the way.

"You up there, Pearson?" you ask. You imagine him in a corner, bat shit all over the shoulders of his jacket.

Regardless of what you imagine, no answer comes from the dark hole in the ceiling.

You pull the pin on the incendiary grenade and pitch it through the hole. It bounces off a support beam, and you lose track of it. Something hisses. It could be a bat. It could be Pearson. It could be escaping gas.

The grenade goes off, and you turn your head away from the blast of white light that shocks all the shadows in the attic.

Hold on. Is standing here a good idea?
Go to 158.

You are ready for anything.
Go to to 162.

143

The path curves. You don't like leaving the security of that stone wall on the other side of the hedge, but you have no choice if you are going to follow the maze. The hedges creep closer. You wonder if you've made a bad choice, and then the path does a hairpin turn and . . .

. . . ends.

"What the hell?" you say. "This is it?"

Archer peers at the hedge in front of you. "No, look," she says. "There's a gap here." She steps forward. There is a crackle of dead branches, and she disappears.

You dart after her, and yes, there is a gap. You force your way through it, and find yourself back at the beginning of the maze.

"Seriously!" You lose your temper. "This is bullshit. What are we doing here?"

Archer cuts you off with an upraised hand. "Someone's crying," she says. "They're in pain."

"Can you please focus a little more this time?" you ask.

"This way," Archer says.
Go to 58.

"No, this way," Archer says. She starts off. You hang back. You're sure you've gone this way before . . .
Go to 60.

144

There comes a time in any job when the malignant presence finally reveals itself. Of course, the trick is to not lose your mind before that. Once the monster shows itself though, you can get down to business.

You reach into one of the many secret pockets of your jacket and pull out your kit. Each Closer's kit is different, but you all have the same basic tools: a ceremonial knife, sulphur, salt, holy water, a Sharpie or two, and an incendiary grenade.

You sprinkle sulphur and salt in a circle around you. Prick your finger for some blood and get that circle churning. While it's heating up, you write down your intent along the edge of the circle. Keep it focused and precise! Then, seal the whole thing with some holy water.

A little flash. A little bang on the eardrums. Now: nothing gets in; very little gets out.

Once your circle of protection is up, you can start the laborious process of Closing. It used to be an eighteen-step process, but in the last few years, Night Office Asset Resource Managament has approved a shorter version. Only elven steps now.

Time to bend your fingers into magical pretzels. Let's get started at the top.

The monster comes out of woodwork at step four, intent on breaking your circle. You pause, and watch it hurl itself at the invisible barrier of your circle for awhile. When it realizes your determination is strong (buttressed, of course, by the first three phrases of the incantation, but it's not smart enough to realize that it should have jumped you earlier), it settles on its haunches to wait for you to make a mistake.

You won't, of course, because you're a professional.

And the way you know your circle will hold is when you pop the pin out of the grenade and roll it between the monster's feet.

It goes off with a nasty bang, and you can't help but flinch when the monster's body is splattered all over the front of your circle of protection.

But none of it gets inside

See? You made a good circle.

Now, let's do the rest of this ritual and Close this place down.

NICE AND TIDY. WELL, EXCEPT FOR ALL THAT MONSTER GOO, SPATTERED ON THE WALLS. BUT THAT'S OKAY. IT'S JUST PROOF YOU DID GOOD.

ASSESSMENT SCORE: 89

Please refer to the Appendix for further information regarding your Assessment Score.

145

You finish your investigation of the house. As a final act, you Close the front door, ensuring that whatever is inside stays inside forever. Well, at least until the city bulldozes the structure into a pile of plaster and kindling. There will probably be some bone and tissue mixed in. Within acceptable ranges, though. You are a professional, after all.

A few weeks later, you are visited by a pair of Auditors who want to talk about Pearson. You tell them most of the truth, which seems to make them happy (as happy as Auditors can ever be, that is). And that's it. The case is filed, and you move on.

The job is like that. Sometimes people disappear. Sometimes you end up imagining them from the get-go. That's what the Audit is for: to vet whether you've lost your mind or not, because that's an issue with this job. Sometimes you start imagining things from the moment you step on-site. Phantoms get real. The other side breaks on through. Sanity can be in short supply.

You'll win this war, eventually. You just have to hold on . . .

SURE, YOU SURVIVED, BUT NO BONUS POINTS WILL BE AWARDED FOR SUCH MERELY SERVICEABLE WORK.

ASSESSMENT SCORE: 70

Please refer to the Appendix for further information regarding your Assessment Score.

146

You and Archer walk into a clearing that is filled with bones. "This is weird," Archer says. "It's like a graveyard or—"

And then a lion eats her.

THIS ENDING IS PROBABLY INFURIATING. IT IS, HOWEVER, AN HOMAGE TO THE LITERARY WORK OF WILLIAM SYDNEY PORTER, WHO WAS—IN HIS OWN WAY— AN ADHERENT TO THE TRUTH OF COSMIC INDIFFERENCE. LIFE MERELY ENDS, SOMETIMES. THERE IS NO PLAN. THERE IS NO REASON. OH, WELL.

ASSESSMENT SCORE: 50

YOU MAY BE INCLINED TO ARGUE THAT SUCH AN ENDING DENIES YOU AGENCY. THAT IS A VALID ARGU- MENT. PRESENT YOUR CASE TO THE PROCTOR; THEY MAY ADJUST YOUR SCORE.

Please refer to the Appendix for further information regarding your Assessment Score.

147

You storm through the rest of the house. Nothing stands a chance.

There's something dark and wiggly in a cedar chest upstairs, but you Close the chest before it can jump out at you.

The attic is filled with poison-fanged bats, but you Close the space up so tight they expire in less than thirty seconds from a lack of oxygen.

Even the basement with its fang-mouthed boiler and sticky floors doesn't slow you down. You are the Closer, and this site is going to submit to your will.

The front door is still jammed when you are finished, which is infuriating. Some of your ire bleeds off as you have to reverse-engineer a spell to unbind the latch. Intricate puzzles requiring a delicate touch are tough when your brain is yelling, "Burn it all down!"

Eventually, the latch yields. The house collapses in on itself as you walk away. Dramatic exit? Check.

You find Archer waiting by the cars. "Took you long enough," she says, looking up from her phone.

"I had to deal with an unexpected snag," you say.

She raises an eyebrow. "I take it Pearson didn't make it?"

"He didn't."

She shrugs and puts her phone away. "Spike trap?"

"Space jelly," you tell her.

Archer shudders. "I hate space jellies."

"There's one less of them now."

"Nice." She offers you a fist bump. "We'll get them all, eventually."

You bump her fist, and then both of you do the floating octopus kiss-off.

"Eventually," you say.

It'll probably take a million years, but that makes for job security, right?

FIST BUMPS ARE AN APPROPRIATE CELEBRATORY GESTURE. YOUR RAGE IS GOOD, TOO.

ASSESSMENT SCORE: 85

Please refer to the Appendix for further information regarding your Assessment Score.

148

Archer is waiting for you in the foyer.

"Where's Pearson?" she asks. Her eyes are bright. You know she's been staring too long into the Way.

"I'm not sure," you say. "It's like the house swallowed him."

"You think they popped his brain or something?"

"Or something," you say.

Archer gnaws on her lower lip. She looks at the stairs without seeing them, a tension line furrowing across her forehead. She's peering through the veils of time and space, glimpsing possibilities and finalities.

"Oh," she says.

Her forehead creases more.

"We should go," she says.

You know better than to argue with an operative who has just taken a peek into the Way. You follow her out of the house, and she quickly shuts the door behind you. Before she asks, you fuse the lock shut so the door won't open again.

"Good timing," she says.

And something slams into the other side of the door.

"Lurker," Archer says. "I saw it coming."

The door rattles again.

"Did it get Pearson?" you ask.

"It *is* Pearson," she says.

"Ah, one of those." So much makes sense now.

A tight smile creases her lips. "That's good work," she says, nodding toward the lump of metal that used to be the latch and locking mechanism. "It should hold."

"*Should?*"

She shrugs. "I'm not going to look that far. That'll lock it in. It's better to have options." She starts off across the lawn. "Time to call it in," she says over her shoulder.

With a last look at the door of the foreboding mansion, you follow Archer back to her car. Behind you, the thing that used to be Pearson keeps pounding at the door. You know your seal will hold.

You're not so sure about the door itself . . .

IT IS IMPORTANT TO KNOW WHEN TO CALL DISPOSAL. SOMETIMES CONTAINMENT IS ENOUGH.

ASSESSMENT SCORE: 76

Please refer to the Appendix for further information regarding your Assessment Score.

149

Archer is waiting for you in the foyer. She notices your expression. "You find something?" she asks.

"Something found me," you say.

"You? What about Pearson?"

You shake your head, and she frowns.

You shine your flashlight up the stairs. "One more floor."

Archer indicates you should go first, and you take the lead.

There's another shoggoth hiding in a cedar chest in the closet of the master bedroom. Archer senses it before she even enters the room. You Close the chest before it can jump out at either of you. The ease with which you deal with this monster makes you aware that the three of you should have never split up. The team works together. The Opener opens, the Way sees, and the Closer puts things to rest. That's the way it has worked for centuries. That's the only way it will continue to work.

The reason Pearson died is because he broke the trinity. He stepped out of the triangle.

"It's always the Openers," Archer says later as the two of you are heading toward your cars. The Zelphepjer House is a black box behind you, its horrors sealed away for all eternity. "They get too eager."

You don't disagree; you just wish there was another way.

NO ONE EVER SAID THIS JOB WAS GOING TO BE 'FUN.'

ASSESSMENT SCORE: 77

> Please refer to the Appendix for further information regarding your Assessment Score.

150

You should have some glowsticks in one of your pockets. You fish around for awhile, trying to remember where you stashed them. You find an old pastry from last week, which is embarrassing, but not so embarrassing that your stomach doesn't let you know that you should hang on to it.

Ah, there they are.

You snap and shake three of them. Once they activate, you lob them around the room. Past the scrap pile. Behind the furnace. You miss the well with the third, but that's okay because it was a long shot anyway. The glowsticks make shadows, which is better than all that inky darkness you were dealing with. You keep sweeping the room with your flashlight beam, hoping the combination of glowstick and flashlight beam will reveal where Pearson is hiding.

Ping. Ping.

You shine the light at the furnace. It's capacity is excessive for a house this size. You could fit a lot more than a bucket full of coal in that thing . . .

The tapping noise is coming from the hulking shape. The sound of metal on metal.

You think of the finger caps of Pearson's Hand.

Ping.

You sidle along the wall, moving cautiously until you can peek around the furnace. Your glowstick paints the side with a greenish patina. Nobody is crouching behind the metal box.

The pinging noise continues to taunt you. *Why can't you find me?* the noise says. *I'm right here. Right in front of you.*

You know you are imprinting an intelligence on the noises. They aren't calling to you. They're just the sound metal makes when it taps on metal. It's not a secret code. It's not hypnotizing you . . .

Oh God! What if it is hypnotizing you?
Go to 155.

That noise has to be coming from inside the furnace.
Go to 153.

151

It has been a long night, and you are feeling a bit parched. If Pearson is waiting to ambush you, he's not going anywhere. Surely, you have a minute or two to chill, right?

Your search in your pockets for a wine opener. It's a little out of character for you to be carrying such a useful tool, but you have yet to meet an Opener with enough control and dexterity to not send glass flying everywhere when they open a bottle of wine. And how many times have a bunch of operatives stood around after a successful job and looked glum because no one thought to bring a wine opener?

Too many.

You allocated some pockets for practical things. Not everything has to be job-related and death-dealing. It's important to be well-rounded.

Anyway, you find the opener and slice off the top of the foil. The cork is still intact, and you pull it out without too much trouble. The bottle makes a gentle pop, but nothing made of space jelly or undying darkness come shooting out.

You realize you didn't pack a glass, and there isn't one behind the bar. Oh well, you might as well drink straight from the bottle. It's not like you were going to share it with anyone else.

It's a good year, the Old Man says. *Light and crisp. You can't even taste the rot.*

Rot? You lower the bottle. *What rot?*

He's in the mirror, looking back at you. *Botrytis cinerea*, he says. *It's a type of fungus that grows on the grapes. They cultivate it. Can you believe that? They call it 'noble rot.' It makes the grapes sweeter, apparently.*

So it's poisoned by design? You raise the bottle and take another sip, which is odd because you had a vague sense that you should be a little more careful.

The whole world is poison, the Old Man says.

You glare at him. *No one misses your tired cynicism*, you think.

He gives you a patronizing smile. When he lifts his hand, you see that he is holding a flare gun. *Drink up*, he says, and when you raise the bottle again, he mimics you, putting the barrel of the flare gun in his mouth. *The job's almost done.*

The bottle tastes funny. Almost metallic.

In the mirror, the Old Man winks at you.

As he pulls the trigger, you realize there never was any bottle of '62 Chateau d'Qyeure. You're all alone in the basement of the Zelphepjer estate. That's not the Old Man in the mirror. That's you.

Like it did with Pearson, the house finally got inside your head.

The hammer drops, and the gun goes off . . .

THE HUMAN MIND IS SO EASILY LED ASTRAY. REMEMBER THIS FOR NEXT TIME.

ASSESSMENT SCORE: 40

Please refer to the Appendix for further information regarding your Assessment Score.

152

You keep going down the stairs. You have to finish this. There's no one else. Besides, by the time you get clear and make contact with the Night Office, who knows how many batrachian bottom-feeders could come through whatever portal is being opened down in the basement.

You know that's why they grabbed Pearson. Miss Eliza couldn't finish the Great Summoning, and whatever managed to get through ate her brain. All that was left was that bleak emptiness—that great cosmic loneliness that swallows you whole—and it wanted to feel something again. It wanted to bring the rest of its brood into this world too, and to accomplish that, it needed an Opener.

The air gets thicker, and you feel like you are breathing soup. The beam of your flashlight barely illuminates two steps beyond where you are standing. You should be counting steps, but you've lost track. You feel like you are underwater. Sweat is pooling in the collar of your jacket. It's getting warmer too.

And then, suddenly, you're at the bottom of the stairs.

You wave the flashlight around, and all you see is darkness.

Your breath is heavy in your throat. Sweat drips off your eyelashes.

Hazard pay, you tell yourself. *This is worth some serious hazard pay.*
Go to 154.

Maybe this is a bad idea, you think.
Go to 157.

153

You approach the furnace warily. There is a metal grate on the front. You shine your light through the bars, and light reflects back, like when you surprise a raccoon at the dumpster behind your apartment building. There's something in the furnace, and you instinctively reach for the handle on the heavy door, but catch yourself in time.

You shine the light inside again. "Pearson?"

He's curled up, arms wrapped around his stomach. There's dried blood on the side of his head. His face is slick with sweat. He raises his head when you call out his name a second time. "It's in me," he whines. "I can feel it in my head."

"What is it?" you ask.

He shivers. Or maybe he shakes his head and the rest of him follows suit. You're not sure. It doesn't matter.

"I can't hold it for long," he says. "It's going to take over again." He jackknifes suddenly, his boots striking the door with a clang. He spasms a few more times with lessening intensity, and then he goes limp.

You shine the light on the instrument panel. There are some new gauges and switches, suggesting the unit was converted to natural gas at some point. Coal isn't cool anymore, after all.

"I can get an Extraction team down here," you say.

He laughs quietly at your lie. "You gotta turn it on," he says. "It's the only way."

"Yeah, I don't like that sort of talk," you say.

"You'd ask the same of me," he says, and you look away. He's right, and you'd be less generous about him waffling than he is with you.

"One of us needs to get out," he says.

"That's not how it works," you protest. "We open; we find the way; we close. That's how it works. That's the rule of three."

"*You* close," he whispers. "That's the only rule that matters."

He's not wrong, the ghost of the Old Man says. *What did I teach you?*

God damn it, you think.

That's not what the Old Man taught you, but that's the sentiment to remember, nonetheless. It's all damned. It's all destined to be burned for all eternity. No one escapes. The only hope anyone has is to go quickly when your time comes. To be yourself when you die. To know that you stayed human to the end.

You reach over and twist the dial that controls the temperature of the furnace.

Pearson groans, a low noise that turns to a hiss, and you know he's losing the fight for his mind.

"I'm sorry," you say.

DO IT!" he shouts suddenly. His eyes are wide and staring. The veins are standing out in his neck.

You flip the switch that releases gas into the furnace. It reaches the pilot light in the base of the burn box, and ignites.

IT IS OKAY TO LOOK AWAY. ANYONE WITH AN OUNCE OF COMPASSION WOULD.

ASSESSMENT SCORE: 66

Please refer to the Appendix for further information regarding your Assessment Score.

154

NIGHT OFFICE ASSET RESOURCE MANAGEMENT EMPLOYEE GUIDE.

[8.12] ADDITIONAL PAY.
Under no circumstances does the Night Office offer, imply, or otherwise made available additional compensation, financial rewards, "spiffs," bonuses, gifts, or other largesse that may or may not be reported as taxable income beyond the basic compensation package as an incentive for operatives to act outside official guidelines, mission parameters, and other safety regulations. No executive officers of the Night Office will make any such offer for extended compensation based on performance (or lack, thereof) of any operative at any time during a designated job.

The Night Office does not entice, induce, cajole, threaten, or otherwise pressure an operative to perform an action or series of actions that might threaten their lives or sanity or the fabric of the known universe.

The Old Man liked to quote the whole section about additional pay during training. *In other words*, he would sum up, *we won't slip you a little extra on the side, because we know it's a lie. More money does not mean a better chance of survival. It only means you're going to do something stupid, and the Night Office is not in the stupidity business.*

It became a code phrase. "I'm going for hazard pay" indicated an awareness of the statistical probabilities that were in play. That all members of a team should be paying close attention to what each other was doing, because sometimes these abominations were clever enough to hide in plain sight. Sometimes their influence was subtle, and you didn't realize your partner wasn't human any more until it was too late.

And sometimes, when the rational part of your brain was screaming "Holy fuck! Why aren't you running?", that was when you really were tested. When you found out if you were strong enough to do the job.

And, well, here's hoping, right?

Having second thoughts? No one would blame you, really,
Go to 159.

Still determined to get this "hazard pay"?
Go to 160.

155

You shake off the idea that the seemingly random and sporadic *tap-tap-tap-tap* is actually hypnotizing you. You will cop to exhaust and paranoia, but you're not about to get hypnotized by bells, for crying out loud. You're a professional. You've had extensive training in withstanding hypnogogic suggestion and mesmerification. You can count backward from one thousand, skipping every third number. If that doesn't—

Wait a minute. "Mesmerification." Is that even a word?

It must be. The word was in your head a minute ago, and you didn't need to run to a dictionary, so—context! You figured out what it was from context! Even if you didn't know the definition of the word, you understood it—

Ugh. This is confusing. What were you doing? Oh, right. Looking for that missing girl. She had a journal—

Wait. What journal? You didn't find a journal, did you?

Oh, it must be over here. In this closet.

No. It's not a closet. It's something else.

You pause for a moment. There's something important you had to remember. What was it?

Oh, well, it'll come to you in a minute. You just need to crawl into this closet—no, this *casket*. That's right. This *metal* casket.

Basket. It rhymes with basket. That's what you were trying to remember.

No, that wasn't it either. Shit. Something's not right.

I'll say, you giggle. You'll the one who has a possessed gargoyle at home. *Something is definitely not right.*

A metal grate swings shut and you stare at it blankly.

Why does this casket have a grate on it?

Why are you *in* a casket?

And then the eldritch influence vanishes, and you are yourself again.

Fuck. You just crawled into the furnace.

There's a hissing sound, and you smell gas. Gas? You thought this was a coal-burning furnace.

It used to be, a very precise voice says in your head. It's not the Old Man's voice. It's not your mother's voice. It's your voice, but so very world-weary and tired. *They converted it to gas more than a decade ago, when coal went out of vogue.*

Something eclipses the light from outside the furnace. It's Pearson—well, it used to be Pearson. Now it is something wearing Pearson's skin—and badly, at that. It grins at you, and you hear a *whoomp!* as the gas hits the pilot light underneath you . . .

YOU'RE PROBABLY WONDERING WHAT HAPPENED. MARK THIS FEELING. IT USUALLY SWEEPS OVER A FIELD AGENT SHORTLY BEFORE THEY DIE. MARK IT, AND LEARN TO FEAR IT.

ASSESSMENT SCORE: 42

Please refer to the Appendix for further information regarding your Assessment Score.

156

Keeping your flashlight trained on the murk, you back up slowly until you reach the top of the stairs. Nothing comes up after you, either, which is a relief.

You head back to the foyer and try the front door. It's still stuck, and you don't waste any time on it. You go out the same way you came in, worming your way through the gap you made in the plywood covering the sitting room windows.

When you are outside, you take a few deep breaths, enjoying the night air. Night Office operatives don't last long if they are the slightest bit claustrophobic, and you never showed any inclination for that psychological condition. Thankfully, because there were a few moments in that hidden stairway when you could feel the walls closing in.

You go back to your car and make the call.

Desk Management takes down your job ID and the address of the Zelphepjer estate. You make your report, and they give nothing away when they repeat the highlights back to you. Desk Management does not judge. Desk Management is only there to route information from one location to another.

"I need backup," you say.

"Heavy Battery or Clean Sweep?"

"Heavy," you say. *Why fuck around?*

"One moment," Desk Management says. You nod, even though they can't hear you, and stare out the windshield, only half-listening to the minimalist ambient drone that serves as hold music.

You start to feel some of the bruises from the evening, and imagine you're going to look like a fright tomorrow. You're lean over and rummage around in the glove box for some ibuprofen.

Desk Management comes back on the line. "Heavy in-bound," they say. "ETA is thirty minutes. Can you contain until then?"

You duck your head and peer at the top corner of the house that is visible beyond the hedge. You don't see black fire or foul smoke. "Yeah," you say. "I can wait."

"Very good," Desk Management replies. Since there isn't anything else to report, Desk Management hangs up, and you're left alone with your thoughts.

You manage to keep the cynicism at bay.

Twenty-eight minutes later, a black panel van pulls up in front of the house, and five people wearing electric yellow jumpsuits climb out. They haul a bunch of black cases out of the back of the van. They gear up: backpacks, hoses, snorkel masks, long-snouted weapons. One of the them looks in your direction and throws a quick salute. *Heavy Battery is here.*

You flash your headlights in acknowledgment. You've been dismissed. Heavy Battery is going to take care of things now. You don't bother to stick around and see what happens next.

You stop at the liquor store on the way home, and get another bottle of gin. Mr. Fish ate the last one, and you're going to need a stiff drink or two or six tonight.

Tomorrow, there will be a lot of paperwork.

CALLING IN HEAVY BATTERY IS A NIGHT OFFICE ASSET RESOURCE MANAGEMENT APPROVED SOLUTION. IT DOES, HOWEVER, MEAN EXTRA PAPERWORK.

ASSESSMENT SCORE: 79

Please refer to the Appendix for further information regarding your Assessment Score.

157

You find your flare gun in your pockets, and you point and shoot it into the darkness. There's all sorts of comforting light and noise when the gun goes off. You expect the flare to hit a wall, but it doesn't. It just flies off and vanishes, as if it was swallowed by a whale.

"Okay, then," you say. You can take a hint.

You turn around and head back up the stairs. The temperature keeps climbing, and each step feels like it is adding another thirty kilos or so to your shoulders. You trudge and trudge. Are you getting anywhere? Why didn't you count the steps? You chide yourself, though you know such admonishment isn't quite fair. There were a lot of steps, and they all looked the same. Besides, you are awfully tired, and this job is so hard.

You frown at that thought. That isn't like you. Sure, cynicism comes with the job, but that's usually applied to the rest of humanity. You know your job. You know how hard it is. This is—

The air is poisonous. It's killing your brain cells, and every moment you stay down here is bringing you that much closer to the brink of fatalistic ennui.

You slap your leg with the flashlight. *Don't stop*, you tell yourself. *Keep moving. Don't let them win.*

Your foot is so heavy. Your back aches. *How much further? Keep moving!*

Your foot moves slowly.

Keep moving!

In your desperation to break free of the entropic lassitude that is stealing your will to live, you trip over the edge of the next step. As you break your fall with your hands, you drop your flashlight. It bounces off the nearest step and rolls downstairs. You can only stare in horror as the light gets fainter and fainter.

And then it is gone.

The darkness is all around you. It's pushing down on you. It gets in your lungs when you suck in a breath. Yes, you are sucking more of it in now, aren't you? You are panicking. You want to scream. You want to run, but you can't run up the stairs. You can't even get up. Your foot is stuck. Why is your foot stuck? God, it's so hard to breath. Everything is so heavy.

I'm just going to rest here a minute, you think, *and then I'll try again.*

Just a . . .

. . . *minute* . . .

. . . *wait . . . how long?*

NOT ALL OF THE DEATHS IN THIS TRAINING MANUAL ARE QUICK.

ASSESSMENT SCORE: 44

Please refer to the Appendix for further information regarding your Assessment Score.

158

Something starts thrashing in the attic. Wood and insulation and something that smells like wet rabbit and carrion are all on fire. A loud thud shakes the ceiling, and you hastily back up to the doorway of the room.

Flaming chunks of wood and smoking insulation come tumbling down as the ceiling breaks. Something with shriveled wings and tentacles comes down too. It rolls around on the floor, trying to put out the streamers of fire licking its misshapen body.

It is wearing leather boots. It's not much of a stretch to guess that this was Pearson once. Now, it's just some monster caught up in a Darwinian evolutionary game. *I'm a bird! I'm an octopus! I'm on fire!*

Once-Was-Pearson manages to put out the fires. He crawls at you, his ragged beak of a face gaping and clicking. His tentacles shed their burned flesh as they enlongate.

It might be fascinating to watch the time-lapse transformation if the monster wasn't intent on eating you as soon as it developed enough mouths to do so.

You find that jar of naphtha you carry for when the time for politeness has passed. You hurl the jar at Once-Was-Pearson, and it shatters against his head.

Once-Was-Pearson makes even more noise, and the sound is really terrifying. The more he screams, the more human he sounds. He's almost making real noises now. Trying to say your name. Trying to beg for help.

You gingerly grab the door knob. It's hot to the touch, and you give it a quick jerk.

"Sa—sa—sa—save meeeee," Pearson sobs. You look back, and it's mostly him now. The naphtha is a lake of fire around him. He's crying as he reaches out to you. "Pleeaaaseeee . . ."

His fingers are too long, and his tears are black.
You shake your head and pull the door all the way shut.
And then you Close the room.

THE NIGHT OFFICE CONSIDERS BEING A COLD-HEARTED PROFESSIONAL A VALUABLE CHARACTER TRAIT IN THEIR FIELD OPERATIVES.

ASSESSMENT SCORE: 86

Please refer to the Appendix for further
information regarding your Assessment Score.

159

Fuck this, you think. It's time to get out before something eats your brain. You turn tail and bolt up the stairs.

You might even have made it too, if you hadn't paused on the top step to catch your breath.

You thought you were far enough away from whatever was in the basement, but all that heavy air you breathed while you were down there? It wasn't just air. It was filled with spores— little baby space jellies.

What happens next is that you find yourself short of breath. Understandable, perhaps, given the total panic dash you just made. But that shortness doesn't go away. Your heart starts pounding harder, in fact, and there's a voice in your brain that is shouting about a lack of oxygen. Odd, really, because you are sucking in a lot of air, aren't you? But none of it seems to be getting to your bloodstream.

That's because your lungs are filling up with fungi.

You collapse and cough up something that looks like a scrap of honeycomb. All that's left is for you to suffocate on the floor of the old library.

Gasping like a fish out of water . . .

THIS ENDING HAS EXTRA STING FOR THOSE WHO DON'T LIKE SOUP. YOU'RE NOT ONE OF THOSE PEOPLE, ARE YOU?

ASSESSMENT SCORE: 34

Please refer to the Appendix for further information regarding your Assessment Score.

160

Of course, at a certain point, you're just going to push ahead because you want the cred. You want to be able to stand in the break room and say, "So, yeah, I Closed the Zelphepjer portal." And everyone will clap, and there will be whispers and stares later, because you—yes, *you*—went down into the basement and did the job that no one else could do. And you did it because it had to be done.

Any one of you would have done the same, you'll say, and everyone will nod and make agreeable noises, but none of them will look you in the eye. You won't care, because—for a little while—you can ride the mystique of being *that* daredevil.

That's the Old Man's secret, isn't it? The one he told you when he found out about Mr. Fish. *I did something stupid once*, he told you, *because I was young and an idiot, and because I didn't want to be the guy who flinched. Who ran away from the gibbering horrors when I came face to face with them. No one told me that we were supposed to run away. But I didn't and I lived, and now everyone thinks I'm some kind of inhuman badass.*

Maybe I was, he said. *In that moment, maybe I was. But, afterward? That feeling never lasts . . .*

Something shuffles in the darkness, interrupting your train of thought. Don't forget to actually finish what you came here to do, okay? You're in a basement where all the light has fled. Where hope is bleeding out. Where there is a yawning portal to an infinite void of cold emptiness.

There's some comfort in knowing you aren't alone, isn't there? Regardless of whether or not it is human, there is other life down here. It wants to eat you, and that's okay, because you want to send it screaming back to the cold place where it came from. You aren't going to be friends—you and whatever loathsome tentacled spawn of some obscene god is in here with you.

That's okay. You have Mr. Fish. He's all the friends you need, really.

You take out the Elder Sign from one of your pockets and slip it into your mouth. It tucks in nicely against your cheek. You tongue gets tingly, and the stone's warmth spreads to your throat.

Come on, star slime, you think. *Let's do this.*

ALL FIELD AGENTS SHOULD ALWAYS STRIVE TO STRIKE FEAR INTO THEIR ENEMIES. IT MAKES FOR GOOD PR.

ASSESSMENT SCORE: 90

Please refer to the Appendix for further information regarding your Assessment Score.

161

You yank open the door on the right, and it's an empty linen closet. Of course! You should have realized this was what you'd find. This is the inside wall. There's a big open space nearby where the staircase runs down to the foyer.

Annoyed about the state of your mental map, you shake your head and close the linen closet door.

Pearson is standing in the hall less than a meter from you.

You have a brief moment to shine the light in his face. All you see are his dead eyes and the way his lips are stained with darkness. He shrieks like a bandsaw as he lunges, his Hand reaching for your face. You block his attack with your flashlight. He grabs it, along with your fist. You try to shake him off before he can—

His Hand pulses, and the flashlight deconstructs itself. All of its seams split, and the tiny screws go shooting off. The batteries explode. The LED bulbs pop. Unfortunately, your hand gets Opened too. Your knuckles melt. Finger bones fall off.

You try not to scream. That's what he wants. The sound will create a harmonic vibration that will resonante through your body. The rest of your cells will try to Open too.

You've seen it happen. It's not pretty.

You pull your wrecked hand free of his grip and stagger away. You start blabbering. Incoherent phrases. Random number sequences. Anything to keep a rhythm from developing—it's the verbal equivalent of St. Herbert's Shuffling Step.

Pearson's Opening, unable to build its harmonic, fades. You're not going to lose any more flesh and bone.

Leaning against the wall, your ruined hand thrust between your legs, you stare at Pearson. Getting a read on the thing that has devoured him and is now wearing his skin.

It stands loosely in the hall, swaying from side to side. "Do you know me?" it asks. It's voice is all wrong for a human.

Your core temperature is falling. You're going into shock. You need to do something quick.

"I know evil when I see it," you say.

You have a phosphorus grenade in one of your hidden pockets for situations like this. The casing has been thrice-blessed, which makes the even the tiniest piece of it deadly. You fumble with your jacket, trying to find the right pocket. Your mangled hand is making this a little tough.

The monster cocks Pearson's head in a strangely bird-like manner. It doesn't seem to be in a rush to devour you.

They're not the brightest bulbs in the universe, thank God.

It focus on the metal object you produce from your coat. It licks Pearson's lips. "Fun box," it says.

"Fuck you," you reply. There's a zero second delay on this grenade. No point in trying to get clear when you use it. It's a last-ditch solution.

You jerk the pin out with your thumb and release the hammer. A bright—

NIGHT OFFICE ASSET RESOURCE MANAGEMENT APPRECIATES YOUR SACRIFICE, BUT REALLY, THEY WERE HOPING YOU WOULD MAKE IT BACK. IT'S MORE COST EFFECTIVE THAT WAY.

ASSESSMENT SCORE: 67

Please refer to the Appendix for further information regarding your Assessment Score.

162

The incendiary grenade illuminates God knows what up there. Dust. Bats. Insulation. Something withered and dry. You hear bumping and thrashing noises, which sound like something is not happy.

A crack appears in the ceiling, and you realize you might be too close to the action.

Suddenly, the ceiling breaks. Chunks of flaming wood and smoking insulation come raining down. That's not all that comes down; there's something monstrous, too. Something that had been human once, but which has been stretched and turned inside out. It has tentacles and beaks now.

It's on fire, too, which makes for an awesome spectacle as it crashes into the room. Some other time you might admire the show, but whatever it is isn't dead. In fact, it's very much alive and very pissed off.

It's a good thing you weren't standing underneath it, right? Even better that you're already halfway out the room. Operational prudence suggests putting even more space between you and it. As the monster thrashes about in the mess of burning plaster, you shuffle backward into the hall.

Where you run into something.

"What the hell?"

It's Pearson, and he's blocking the hall.

"Get out of—"

Only then do you notice his eyes are dead. His mouth is gaping open, like he doesn't know how to work the muscles in his jaw.

The creature in the room has gone quiet, which means it has focused on you. You smell burning flesh and feathers. *Why does it even have feathers?* you start to wonder, but there's no time to ask that question, much less hear an answer.

You're about to be a snack for a trans-dimensional bird thingie. Your last thought is you don't recall this being one of the choices in the Night Office "How Are You Likely To Die?" pool.

That's vexing. A win in the office pool would have kept Mr. Fish in kibble and sausages for quite some time. Instead . . .

NO, YOU DIDN'T WIN THE OFFICE POOL.

ASSESSMENT SCORE: 52

Please refer to the Appendix for further information regarding your Assessment Score.

163

The altar is made from pieces of dark stone that have been artfully shaped so that gravity holds them in place. The top piece is longer than it is wider, and there's a groove that runs along the rim. On one end, there's a hole in the stone about the size of a quarter. Underneath, there is another hole in the floor, which is large enough for your fist. You're not stupid enough to put your hand down there, especially when you notice the spatter stains around the hole in the floor. It's a drain, you realize. *But where does it go?*

There are nicks and scrapes on the altar, which suggests rituals with knives. Whoever was doing the cutting wasn't too careful . . .

Something falls heavily, and it takes you a minute to realize what the sound is. The trapdoor!

You race back through the tunnel, and when you get to the ladder, your worst fear is realized: the trapdoor is closed. How could this happen? You scramble up the ladder, and shove at the door. It doesn't budge.

"Archer!" you yell. "Archer! What the fuck is going on?"

You strain to hear anything, but the trapdoor is thick enough that no sound gets through. You pound on the hatch until your hand hurts, but there's no response.

Back in the room, the flare gutters out. The only light left is from the glowsticks scattered at the base of the ladder.

You slide down the ladder, fighting a rising knot of panic. *It fell over*, you think, Archer wandered off and the trapdoor fell over. *That's all. She'll be back.*

The glowsticks go out. Now you can panic.

You scream for awhile, but that only wrecks your throat.

Surely, someone will come looking for you. The Night Office wouldn't leave you here. And what about the rest of your team?

What about them? the Old Man asks.

That's when it sinks in. If your team isn't coming for you, no one is . . .

> **IT WILL TAKE SEVERAL DAYS TO DIE DOWN HERE. THE LAST FEW HOURS WILL BE UNPLEASANT. TRY NOT TO THINK ABOUT THAT.**
>
> **ASSESSMENT SCORE: 53**

Please refer to the Appendix for further
information regarding your Assessment Score.

164

The shadow woman dips her head. Maybe she pouts. It's hard to tell with all the smoke and mirrors. *It's a very sad tale,* she says. *It will make you weep with despair.*

You and Archer fight the urge to roll your eyes.

"Is this your first time?" you ask the shoggoth priestess. "I mean, other than plucking off nubile socialites who don't have the sense of an addled parakeet. If it is, can we cut to the part where we say we don't give a shit about your daddy issues or how no one understands your pain or . . . what was it this year?" The last is directed at Archer.

"Academic under-achievement," she says.

"Right. You failed algebra one too many times, and now you're going to let cosmic darkness overwhelm the world as righteous vengeance for how it has forced math on you."

The shadows spin faster. *You are not as smart as you think you are,* the creature snarls.

"No," you sigh. "I'm not, but I'm smarter than you, so . . ."

The monster streaks out of the gazebo, unfurling into a long banner of tentacles and eyes. You've been expecting some sort of ravenous assault like this, but when it happens, you are still surprised by the creature's speed and ferocity. It doesn't matter how many times it happens; you are never really ready to deal with the unnatural way shoggoths move.

You fall back, your ceremonial knife in your hand. You slash at questing tentacles, shaving off purple tips. The monster shrieks and screams, and throws more tentacles at you.

Archer's no slouch herself, and she forms a wide-bladed hatchet out of the etheric stuff of the Way. Whe she cuts off a tentacle, she takes more than the tip.

You cut and slash with enthusiasm. This is starting to feel like a competition.

The shoggoth has an endless supply of tentacles, though. You're going to have to do something much more dramatic if you're going to show it who is the boss.

You let Archer keep the crawly bits at bay for a minute as you dig in the pockets of your jacket. Where's that portable circle? Ah, there it is. You pull out the folded circle and toggle the switch that lights it up. You unfold it and drop it on the ground. As you step into it, you start chanting the magic spell that activates it.

The shoggoth howls as the circle charges up.

"That's right, you ectoplasmic bowel dripping," you snarl as you reach through thin veil of reality. "It's time to party." Your fingers tingle as the Way makes contact.

The shoggoth knows how to rip reality too. It retreats, but only to turn its tentacles to tearing apart the fabric of this world. The pale hedge maze is replaced by an endless expanse of rippling darkness filled with . . .

Oops. Those aren't stars. They're eyes.

"Oh, shit," Archer breathes. "It's the shoggoth sea."

You've heard about this place. It's what the Old Man referred to as the Primeval Soup. *That first foul squirt from the ass of the Unknownable and Unpronounceable*, he said. Bereft of form and function, this goop was the breeding ground for primal malevolence—that first inkling of fear and desire and rage. The Old Ones found it—maybe they drank from it like desperate wildebeest—and they decanted more of it into sweaty vessels filled with the most incandescent innocence. What thrived in these vessels was fear, fear given form by this black ichor.

When insane philosophers rant about staring into the Abyss and seeing it stare back at them, they're talking about the shoggoth sea. Everywhere you look, it is staring back at you.

As terrifying as this landscape is, you can't help but be drawn in by it. No amount of beauty and truth and human compassion can withstand the deep pull of this sea of shit. Some manage to break free, but they do so only because it lets them. It sends them back so they can whisper stories of what they have seen. They are harbingers of the end, these survivors.

You glance around wildly for Archer. She's farther away than you thought she'd be. Bright birds flash around her. They are distracting her. She's not paying attention to the roiling sewage creeping toward her feet.

One of us will survive, you think. They'll be allowed to return. To tell the tale of what we saw. To warn the rest of humanity about what waits in the beyond. You don't recall deciding what to do, but when you glance down, you realize you've already left your magic circle. You're on blasted ground. There is no going back.

What about Mr. Fish? You have to tell Archer about him. You don't want him to be afraid. He's been hurt enough.

You're almost at the edge of the sea. You fight the cosmic urge to hurl yourself into the malignant swill of cosmic entropy. *Just one more minute*, you think. *Just one—*

"My cat," you shout at Archer.

"What?" She doesn't understand. "You don't have a cat."

"Just think of him as a cat, okay? It's easier that way."

"Who?"

"Mr. Fish—"

Something slides over your foot, and your entire leg goes numb. You struggle for a second, but then the touch of the shoggoth sea reaches your stomach and chest. Your heart stops. You have time for one last, desperate thought.

And—

AND EVERYTHING ENDS. AND NOTHING MATTERS. THESE ARE IMMUTABLE FACTS. YOUR SACRIFICE IS NOTED, THOUGH.

ASSESSMENT SCORE: 74

Please refer to the Appendix for further information regarding your Assessment Score.

165

"The scholar? He disappeared," Archer says as she wanders toward one of paths out of the clearing. "I can't find him in the Way."

"Did he pull a Rasputin, or something?"

"God, no. I could follow that. This is different."

There's an old oak rising out of the ground in the center of the next clearing. It's gnarled and twisted with age. Hanging from its bare branches is a wicker cage.

There's a skeleton in the cage. A human skeleton.

"There's no head," you notice.

"It's missing a hand too," Archer says.

The left hand, in fact, which is the one typically used to make a Hand of Glory. Those sorts of grisly practices went out of vogue a couple of decades ago, though. These days, you've got the Opener rituals. You don't need the mummified hand of a dead murderer anymore. All you need is a little blood magic and a piece of string, frankly.

"This is all really old," you say. "Can you peel back the Way to when he was put up here?"

Archer puts her hand on the trunk of the tree. Overhead, the moon moves backward. The sun comes soon after. They chase each other, going faster and faster until the day and night cycle is an on/off flicker like a kid playing with a light switch. The tree twists and shudders. The wicker cage swings violently.

The blur stops so quickly you get an instant headache from the temporal deceleration. You gasp, and your whole body is covered with a sticky layer of sweat. As you try to orient yourself, you discover you are surrounded by an angry mob.

They aren't solid. You're just a ghost to them, but the sudden presense of all those bodies is still disconcerting. You try to keep your distance, but you keep slipping into people. The more you jerk away, the more you intersect another's space. *Archer,* you cry out. *Damnit, I'm caught in this—*

You look around wildly for Archer. You spot a woman wearing a dark robe. Archer is hovering behind her, out of phase with you, but not with the woman. When the woman moves her arm, Archer mimics her. When the woman shouts at the crowd, it is Archer's voice you hear. "Get back!"

The crowd shuffles closer. Violent thoughts start to boil over in your brain. She's a witch! She summons spirits and ghosts. You've got to stop her.

Archer! Pull free. You have to pull free!

She was moving too fast in the Way, and she got sucked in to a hot spot. You were trailing in her wake, and now you have bonded with this frenzied crowd.

The woman has a ritual knife, and she waves it at the crowd. They recoil for a second, but their mood is too dark—too fixated—and they surge forward. The knife slashes again, and someone gets cut.

You know what is going to happen next. Blood has been shed. *Archer!*

She's merged with the priestess. There's no difference between them now.

The crowd reaches for her. It's lust is your lust now, and you find yourself pushing toward the front. You want your piece of flesh . . .

BENDING TIME IS TRICKY. IT USUALLY DOESN'T GO THE WAY YOU THINK IT WILL.

ASSESSMENT SCORE: 48

Please refer to the Appendix for further information regarding your Assessment Score.

166

"I have backup coming," you say. "We called in Heavy Battery before we starting wandering around this fucking maze. Why do you think we took so long? They had to get in position."

The shoggoth-in-flames flickers. It's not impressed.

You shrug. "Suit yourself, space jelly. I'm warning you. You think you've got my friend here. But she's tapped in. They know how to find her. They're going to flatten you like a dinner roll. After they suck out all you know about the Hierarchy of Awful, they might let you go. Just so the Hierarchs know who told them all their secrets."

Archer stops shivering, but she doesn't come back either. It looks like she's thinking hard.

You tap a glowstick against your knuckles. "What'll it be, stink jam?"

There's a hiss, like air escaping a bicycle tire, and the flame start to dim. When the hiss gets louder, you realize it's coming from Archer's mouth. You wait, fighting the urge to panic. When a full-body shiver runs through Archer, you snap the glowsticks and throw them. They *pop-pop-pop* as they hit the fading fire. You make a grab for Archer before she falls down.

She feels real to you. Real enough, anyway.

"Move," you snarl. You shove her toward the path between the hedges.

She staggers like a drunk, but the training kicks in. She starts moving, and doesn't stop when she reaches the path.

You linger a bit, making sure whatever was peeking through from the Way isn't peeking anymore.

Oh, it is, and it's spitting mad that it has been cheated. But the portal is closing. It can't reverse the process.

You weave a spell with your fingers and words, forcing pressure on the portal from this side. A spike of pain drives into your forehead, bu you ignore it. Psychic force feedback. Occupational hazard. Nothing a bottle of gin won't cure.

The cosmic crawler shrieks once more, but the sound is about as frighening as the shriek of an outraged vole. The air wavers on the far side of the clearing, and then it goes still.

You take off after Archer. Now is definitely the time to call Heavy Battery. They'll rubblize the place properly.

YOU FOUND THE CORE DISTURBANCE AND SUCCESSFULLY NEUTRALIZED IT. YOU HAVE EARNED A PASSING GRADE.

ASSESSMENT SCORE: 91

Please refer to the Appendix for further information regarding your Assessment Score.

167

The creature in the gazebo changes, solidifying in various parts that leave little to the imagination.

"That's, uh—wow," Archer says. She frowns and shakes her head.

You give the well-endowed incubus a thumbs down. 'We're lesbians," you point out. You waggle your thumb at yourself and Archer. "We like other ladies. That"—you indicate the dangling part of the demon—"that's not the lure you think it is."

The cosmic shapeshifter recoils. Eyes scurry over its surface, and it ripples like ocean water blown by the wind as it tries to find another approach.

"Too late," you say. You whip your other hand out from under your coat and let go of the greenish soapstone you had teased out of one of your pockets. It's an Elder Sign. The ones you get from the Night Office armory are more representational than authentic, but with space jellies, it's all about the symbolism anyway.

It tries to get away from the small stone. While it is writhing and swarming, Archer whips out a heavy cloth from her coat pocket and ties it around her head, covering her eyes. The atmosphere crackles through her hair as she descends deep into the Way—God, you'd forgotten how sexy it is when she lets herself go.

You go for your special gear too: glowsticks blessed by the Night Office, the flare gun with the magnesium and phosphorus flares, and the spectral whistle.

The space jelly shrieks through a half-dozen dimensions, calling for other monstrosities that have been lying in wait. You shake and snap a bunch of the glowsticks and scatter them around you and Archer. An over-eager fungi from Yuggoth trips over a glowstick and goes up like a sheaf of dried corn stalks.

Archer splits the sky with crimson lightning bolts. In the flickering light, you see a shifting surf of jellies moving in behind you. "On your right," you warn Archer. She's on it, leaving you to point and shoot at the shoggoth 'shifter in the gazebo.

You fire a flare, and it sparks like a sun going nova. The gazebo fills with shadows that try to snuff out the flare, but oh, darlings, phosphorus burns. It burns so very brightly.

Clamping your teeth around the stem of the whistle, you let loose with a piercing blast that makes the Way tremble. Dogs across six centuries wake and start howling. Cats within a hundred kilometers lose their hair. Something very old twitches in its trench at the bottom of the ocean.

Archer brings the sky down, and everything shatters into a million mirrored shards. You are falling, surrounded by a thousand-year rain. You reach out for her hand, and she finds you. You hold on tight as a black and red tornado sweeps you up. You close your eyes, tap your heels three times—like the old witches used to do—and you land with a thump.

The wind disperses. When you open your eyes, the night is quiet and the lawn is undisturbed.

You are standing in front of the Zelphepjer house. Archer is at your side. Her hair is all messed up, and you imagine yours isn't any better.

The front door of the house opens and Pearson comes out. He starts when he sees you two on the lawn. "I was just—" He closes the door behind him. "I was just finishing up in there."

"Sure," you say. Your voice is ragged, like you've been smoking his nasty cigarettes.

"Didn't find anything," he says. "You two?"

"Oh, just the usual," Archer says casually.

"Cool," he says. He swings his arms back and forth. "You want to, ah, you want to get a drink or something? I mean. Wasn't much here. Seems kind of early to . . ."

You look at Archer, and you see a ghostly image of her clawing lightning down from the sky. "I think we're good," you say. "I, uh, have to go home and feed my cat anyway."

Archer raises an eyebrow. "You don't have a cat," she says.

"What?" Pearson is feeling left out of the conversation.

"I do too," you say.

"I don't believe you," Archer says.

You look at Pearson and shrug. "Whatever." You point at the door behind him. "You lock that?"

"What? Oh, yeah. I locked it."

"Good enough for me," you say. "All right, I'm calling this site Closed. Everyone agree."

Pearson nods.

"Aye," says Archer. "But I still don't believe you about the cat."

"I guess you'd better come over and find out," you say.

There's a twinkle in her eye now. "I guess I'd better."

NOT ONLY HAVE YOU SAVED THE UNIVERSE, BUT YOU APPEAR TO HAVE INVITED YOUR FELLOW AGENT OVER FOR SOME WELL-EARNED PERSONAL TIME OFF. WELL DONE.

ASSESSMENT SCORE: 95

Please refer to the Appendix for further information regarding your Assessment Score.

168

The stone of the plaza is flesh-like in its texture. Fortunately, your permanent marker will write on damn near anything. You start inscribing a circle around the praying goat person. Its voice gets more shrill, and you find it hard to think.

Ash from the fountain keeps falling around you. When a blot of it lands on your wrist, it burns. You ignore the pain and the smell of burning flesh. You have to stay focused.

The goat person's voice makes your nose bleed, but you don't stop.

You finish the circle. Now all you have to do is write out the Closing Ward. *And this*, as the Old Man used to say, *is why you drill and practice.* As your vision starts to blur and more ash burns through your clothing—burning the skin underneath—your hand keeps moving. The sigils squirm, threatening to get away from you, but you keep them in place. You write and write and write, even when you start screaming. When blood fills your throat, you spit it out.

Away from your circle. You're not going to be undone that easily.

The goat person's voice slows down. No, it is time that is slowing down. The silver beads of the fountain turn black. The sun gets bigger.

It's coming, Archer says.

You don't know what it is, and you don't want to know.

You're almost done. Your hand is locked around the pen. Some of the bones in your wrist are exposed. You are leaking from so many places.

Something touches the plaza, and all the stones shake. You are thrown to your knees.

Archer screams.

You don't dare look.

Just one more . . .

You finish the last sigil.

Activating the Ward is easy. There is blood everywhere.

The black sun inverts. The goat person's head explodes. Archer vanishes in a pillar of fire.

You lie down. It seems like the most sensible thing to do now.

The fourth or fifth time you open your eyes, you see Archer peering down at you. It's dark all around, except for a halo surrounding Archer.

"You did it," she says, and when she smiles, you know everything is going to be all right.

EXCELLENT WORK. YOU SHOULD TAKE A FEW DAYS OFF. GO SOMEWHERE WARM AND SUNNY WITH A FRIEND.

ASSESSMENT SCORE: 97

Please refer to the Appendix for further information regarding your Assessment Score.

169

Archer suddenly swings around and leaps at you, her eyes wild and her hands upraised. Oh, shit. The cosmic crawler called your bluff.

You backpedal from the psychic fire, dodging Archer's first attempt to grab you.

You throw a glowstick at her, but it's like tossing a chalkboard eraser at a charging rhino. She catches your hair and pulls hard. "Ow, bitch," you exclaim. You punch her in the armpit, but all she does is look angry and yank again.

Her pain receptors have been turned off. *This isn't good*, you think.

You sweep her leg, and she goes down. But she hangs on to your hair, and you both sprawl in the dirt. It's all elbows, knees, and fingers in eyesockets for a few minutes. You keep holding back from doing any real damage to her body. Oh, God, you're still thinking it is Archer. Are you going to die because you couldn't take down your ex-lover when the shit hits the fan?

This is why the Night Office frowns on relationships between operatives, the Old Man's voice pops into your head, dryly reminds you why there are rules.

You'd like to hit him, but he's dead, and so you take it out on Archer instead. She flinches from your assault, and you get a few seconds to get your shit together.

If you were wearing your other jacket, you'd have a knife hidden in your sleeve, but you opted for deeper pockets tonight instead of clever ones. Wait. You have a claw hammer somewhere, don't you? You tear the lining of your jacket as you get it out. When Archer comes at you again, you smack her on the forehead with the heavy end.

You should have used the other end, a tiny voice protests in your head. You tell it to shut up. *I'm not hurting her*, you insist.

It's got her by the brain stem, the voice says. It sounds like you trying to sound like the Old Man. *There's nothing left of Archer. You've got to kill it. Or it will kill you. Do you want that?*

Archer is staring at you, and when you meet her gaze, her expression softens. "I—" she starts.

It's not her. You know it isn't.

You rush her. You're not listening to what she has to say.

It's not her.

You bring the claw hammer down on her head. And this time, you use the other end.

You yank it out and hit her again. And again.

When Pearson eventually finds you, the rage is all gone. All that is left is a deep and terrible awareness of what you have done.

"I killed her," you sob.

The expression on Pearson's face says it all.

ONLY THE COLD APPLICATION OF FORCE IS SUFFICIENT TO SAVE THE UNIVERSE. THIS IS THE SACRIFICE REQUIRED BY NIGHT OFFICE FIELD AGENTS.

OCCUPATIONAL MENTAL THERAPY AND PSYCHOLOG-ICAL RE-ALIGNMENT TREATMENTS ARE AVAILABLE TO ALL FIELD AGENTS AND ARE PART OF THE CORE BENEFITS PACKAGE OFFERED BY NIGHT OFFICE ASSET RESOURCE MANAGEMENT.

ASSESSMENT SCORE: 77

Please refer to the Appendix for further information regarding your Assessment Score.

APPENDIX: This psychological assessment exercise is a training manual used by Night Office Asset Resource Management. It is intended to establish the viability of candidates for positions in various Night Office Asset Resource Management field and support positions.

Candidates will have received an ASSESSMENT SCORE that reflects the choices and decisions they made during this psychological assessment exercise. This SCORE will be used by Night Office Asset Resource Management recruiters to determine whether to recommend candidates for further evaluation. While assessment scores may not be challenged, candidates may retake this exercise.

An ASSESSMENT SCORE of 'N/A' indicates the candidate has deviated from the spirit of the psychological assessment exercise, and the resultant psychological matrix will be of no use to Night Office Asset Resource Management. However, in demonstrating creative thinking skills, the candidate may be suitable for other occupational opportunities within the Night Office.

A classification of Do Not Hire (DNH) indicates a candidate is not suitable for consideration by the Night Office. No further assessment of this candidate will be considered for one (1) year.

All decisions by Night Office Asset Resource Management are final.

ASSESSMENT SCORE   ARM JUDGMENT

     01 - 20   Unsuitable. DNH.

     21 - 45   Fragile.
              Unlikely to survive
              Orientation.

     46 - 60   Unremarkable.
              Will not provide adequate
              ROI.

     61 - 70   Has potential.
              No one should get their
              hopes up, however.

     71 - 84   Serviceable.
              Not likely to last more
              than five years, though.

     85 - 90   Satisfactory.
              May be resilient enough
              for deep insertion opera-
              tions.

     91 - 99   Excellent.
              Make offer before they
              realize they won't be
              able to unsee what they
              learn.

        100   Highly Creative.
              Thinks outside the box.
              High sense of self-pres-
              ervation. An immpossible
              candidate. Extract imme-
              diately.

CERTIFICATION: Certificates of Completion are available from an automated agent of the Night Office Systemic Knowledge Information Network. Please visit the website and provide your email address and your final ASSESSMENT SCORE. A Certificate of Completion will be sent to you.

You may also receive supplementary training matters that will provide education assistance in light of your final ASSESSMENT SCORE, as well as future communications concerning Night Office recruitment opportunities.

http://www.nightoffice.org/cert/

The Night Office will disavow any public sharing of Certificates of Completion, nor will it comment on the validity of any given candidate's purported ASSESSMENT SCORE.

()   When the opera ends, you wipe your eyes and gather yourself. That was quite the emotional rollercoaster. Why did you wait so long to get tickets? All those voices throughout, and that finale! Incredible.

While you are waiting at the coat check, you run into Lewis and MacCutchins. They look happy together, and the three of you pass in polite conversation until your coats all arrive. You bid them goodnight, and head out of the theater. It's not that far to your apartment, and the sky is clear. You can see the moon winking at you from behind the Pyllandri Building. You throw it a casual salute.

On the way home, you stop at a corner market and get some canned tuna for Mr. Fish. Whistling pleasantly, you cross Nortgutt Avenue and head up Randolph. As you walk, something keeps nagging at you. It's like a flap of skin on the roof of your mouth. You can't quite get to it, but you also can't stop teasing it. Was there something else you were supposed to get at the store?

Ah, well, it'll come to you eventually.

As you stand there, wondering what you forgot, a sedan come tearing around the corner of Stemm. There's a flash of light and you start to look, but the car hits you before you can do anything else. Most of your insides burst, and the bag with the can of tuna flies up, up, and . . .

And you never know if it lands, actually, because you died about three seconds after getting squashed by the car.

WE UNDERSTAND THE VERY HUMAN URGE TO PEEK. HOWEVER, THIS IS PROBABLY NOT THE ENDING YOU EXPECTED TO FIND.

Maybe you should start at the beginning.
Go to 1.

CPSIA information can be obtained
at www.ICGtesting.com
Printed in the USA
LVHW010725091219
639881LV00001B/120/P